Waiting On Wendy

TANZANIA GLOVER

TANZANIA GLOVER

Cover Art by Sia Tania of Design Boutique NL

www.tanzaniaglover.com

Fun fact: I **really** wanted this book to be *The Princess and The Frog* entry for The Faded Fairytales, but I decided to leave it as a standalone and let that series remain exclusive to the Logan brothers. Oh and I was literally gonna call it *Frog Bae* too so let's all just be grateful for my change of heart.

Now for most of the people about to read this novel it'll just be another love story before they move on to the next on their ever-growing to-be-read list. But for others the medical condition that I chose to write about here is their daily reality and for some unfortunately it's the thing they or their loved ones did not or may not survive.

Because of this I did my best to write with even more care than usual to capture as realistic a depiction as possible, but of course all of the research in the world will never amount to actually living with this chronic condition. That being said I have decided to donate a portion of my marketing budget to the American Heart Association and if you enjoy this sweet story then I encourage you to also donate if your budget permits.

Enjoy and don't forget to check out the carefully curated music playlist that complements this magical tale!

TANZANIA GLOVER

CLOCKING IN
MARCH 21ˢᵀ

1

Wendy

Even before I'd ever known a single thing about him, I always thought it was funny how most people took heartbeats for granted. They were literally the thing that kept us all alive, but we only really paid them any attention when we found ourselves breathless from taking the stairs or after jump scenes in a scary movie.

Unfortunately for me though I wasn't "most people" because for as long as I could remember I'd never been able to ignore my wild and erratic heartbeat. And just about every second of every minute of every day, I was painfully aware of just how quickly mine could go from keeping me alive to convincing me that I was about to die soon.

For years now I had been joking that I was probably born worried, but that was only because the truth wasn't very far off. From as early as maybe two or three I became very afraid whenever I heard my father's voice.

I suppose that he couldn't help it being naturally gruff, but the fear mainly came from the fact that his speech was often slurred and aggressive from whatever substance he had managed to get his hands on. And growing up and seeing those same hands as the fists that repeatedly hit my mama was most likely the biggest cause of the anxiety that I struggled with well into adulthood.

But it wasn't the only thing.

We moved around…a lot. I was born in Chicago just like my mama, but I didn't really remember much about the city or my maternal side of the family. See while my father was far from the smartest man, after trapping her with a baby he knew that strategically isolating her would be the only way to keep her dependent on him for everything. That meant never staying in the same place for too long lest she form a bond with somebody other than him.

I didn't actually get to call anywhere home until she finally found the strength to get us away from him for good. But that took years and it was too little too late by then because the damage had already been done. Literally every time I was away from her I was worried.

Worried that it might finally be the day my father tracked us down. Worried that one of the many men who harassed her on the streets would hurt her even though she always let them down "nicely". Just plain worried. But it wasn't until age fifteen when I had my first full-blown panic attack.

I remember thinking that I had peed the bed because that's just how wet with sweat it was when I was jolted awake in the middle of the night. And eventually I did actually lose control of my bladder when I realized that my heart felt like it was practically beating out of my chest.

About halfway to the emergency room I finally calmed down some and realized I wasn't having a heart attack, but it was still just the beginning since it would be years and many more episodes before I was properly diagnosed and treated for my panic disorder. During those early days of uncertainty though my mama would just rock and hold me tightly while reminding me that it would be over soon because every storm ran out of rain.

With time, therapy and meds I managed to develop pretty decent coping skills so these days I recognized my triggers and for the most part I could get through things on my own. It was a good thing too because for a while there in my twenties it seemed like I only had myself to count on anyway. And it would be well over a decade before I finally met somebody else who had the same complicated relationship with their heart as I did with mine.

There was really nothing remarkable about the first time I laid eyes on Kellen Turner. In fact there was nothing remarkable about any part of my life at that time. I was back in Chicago and going into my third year working in my Uncle

Jimmy's diner with no real complaints other than needing a good foot rub after long shifts.

That day in particular just so happened to be even longer than usual though because yet again we were down a waitress. And of course that meant Jimmy telling more than asking me to come back in for the dinner rush.

I had just gotten home and began preparing a meal of my own, but I obediently turned right back around since extra hours at least meant extra cash and let's just say my checking account was in no condition to turn down extra cash. Plus dinner shifts every now and then weren't so bad because the customers always drank more and tipped bigger.

As always my commute was quick and painless since I lived in the small apartment right above the diner. From what I'd heard through the family gossip mill also known as my favorite cousin Lena, back in the day Jimmy used to rent it out to single women and let them skip out on paying if they were "nice" to him. But once his wife Paula got hip to his dirty deeds she locked the place up and threw away the key until I needed it since she always did love my mama.

But as much as I didn't like Jimmy's ways or him as a person in general, he had been the only one to come through for me when I was at my lowest a couple years ago. I was broke, being evicted and in a bind like never before with no one to call except for my mama's oldest brother. And asking me how I had gotten to that point would've been a complete waste of time since even I still didn't fully understand how it'd happened.

After graduating high school I'd had my entire life planned down to a tee. I just knew I would be degreed and married with kids by twenty-five. I would have one of those big *Home Alone* houses and go on exotic vacations whenever I wanted. But reality looked a lot different for me after I lost my rock during my second year in college.

Seeing my mama in a casket should have been the hardest day of my life, but it wasn't because I still had nightmares and vivid dreams of witnessing her rich brown skin beaten purple and blue. So to see her lying peacefully in her favorite dress as if she would wake up any minute to get started on dinner, that actually wasn't so bad. Especially considering how many good painless years she got to live after finally leaving my father.

It wasn't until one day during an afternoon psych lecture, for no reason at all, I experienced the worst bout of anxiety of my life. I couldn't talk. I couldn't breathe. I couldn't do anything but dial her number how I had always done when I was scared.

But that time was different because it was the first time I realized she would never again be able to answer and tell me that my storm would soon run out of rain. And I swore every storm since that one seemed like it had a little extra rain that I could never quite shake.

Leaving school wasn't as tough of a decision as I thought it'd be, but that was probably because the university had been the one to show me the door after losing my scholarships from poor grades and spotty attendance. I would have loved to blame that on my continuous issues with anxiety, but I was honestly only there to make my mama proud anyway so the motivation I'd had for higher education was unfortunately buried right alongside her.

The next decade better known as my terrible twenties was a blur of odd jobs, odder roommates and the oddest cities from coast to coast until I finally crashed and burned in south Florida. That's where I had been when Jimmy came to my rescue.

He didn't even care to hear my sob story and believe me it was a good one too. He just bought me a train ticket to Chicago then greeted me at Union Station with an apron and I'd been working for him ever since.

"Wendy, what are you doing back here already? You ain't Kevin Gates, bitch. I know you get tired," Lena cracked on me while she impatiently waited to punch the clock after me. I glanced over my shoulder to see her looking extra dolled up as usual because she did not play about her tips.

When we were reunited two years ago she'd sworn that we were briefly besties as kids, but I had absolutely no memory of it. If it was true though then we had definitely picked up right were we'd left off because her fun personality made work bearable and instantly made Chicago feel like home.

"Jimmy said the new girl just up and quit *for some reason*," I said sarcastically as I went to tie my apron around my waist since we both knew the real deal.

"Which one? Red Locs or Blonde Fro?" she asked since we didn't even bother learning names or getting attached until they were around for a couple pay periods.

It seemed like the moment Jimmy put his name on the building in the nineties the diner had *somehow* gotten a reputation as the perfect place for pretty girls to make fast cash. After dark on weekends you would have thought this was a strip club or a church the way everybody was in there trying to get saved.

Meanwhile I just wanted to save my damn self to be able to restore the diner to where it had been when my great-grandma Mae first bought it. Back then it was called Mae's Kitchen and it was known for being one of the first stops for folks coming up here from the south. And then of course they kept coming back because it was one of the few spots where they could enjoy the kinds of food they were missing from home since their new city jobs kept them from cooking as much.

Nowadays though we basically only served breakfast, burgers and wings since Jimmy said soul food cost too much and took too long to cook. I was still astounded at how with one snap of his cheap, little bony fingers he'd singlehandedly turned a well-respected eatery into basically diner Hooters with a vintage twist. And the fact that he insisted on making our skirts as short as the checks he gave us didn't exactly attract the same caliber of customers either.

He claimed that we wore the same blush pink uniforms from the fifties and sixties, but I had seen photos of my mama working here as a teenager and the neckline had been lowered to show cleavage and the hem certainly lost a few inches. And of course in a place like this showing a little skin was akin to "asking for" a certain kind of attention anyway.

That was why I preferred working mornings and afternoons because I got to avoid the wild side of Jimmy's that came with the nighttime younger male customers. The only uncomfortable part I had to endure with the early bird special crowd was somebody occasionally forgetting their teeth behind. And I would take that over drunk groping any day.

"Oh sorry. I think it was Red Locs," I said after Lena had repeated her question to me. "He called her in his office right before I left so you already know the rest." She nodded then gave me a knowing look before reaching for her apron.

Around here the two of us were considered lucky because we didn't have to get *initiated* like everybody else, but I wouldn't exactly call anything lucky about being blood relatives with a man like Jimmy.

"I swear the second they're ready to MeToo his ass I'm gonna be right there cheering them on," I told her in all seriousness, but she just laughed to herself.

"Jimmy's old ass being carried out of here in handcuffs like Cuba Gooding Jr. would make my day, but I know that nasty fool would sooner stroke out than be held accountable."

"Yeah you're probably right," I mumbled more to myself, but it still didn't stop me from wondering who would run the diner if that were to ever happen. It wasn't like Jimmy had any kids to pass it down to and surely Paula didn't want the headache so knowing that I was at least in the running was a pleasant thought.

But before I let myself get too deep into thought about a diner style coup d'état, I decided to instead get back out front since the old-fashioned route of hard work would likely be the only way I could ever call myself owner.

The Thursday night dinner rush had just been starting when I'd left a half hour before, but it was now in full swing with every booth and table filled and a butt was in every seat at the counter. A big game was also on so it was even louder than usual. I took one last deep breath, forced a wide smile then grabbed my menus because I could already tell this would be a long one.

But as strange as it might've sounded, working in a high-stress environment was actually really good for my anxiety. I always thought it was probably because it distracted me from my own personal stressors and at least in the diner there was always a fix for a problem which was more than I could say for non-work issues.

Yeah that was probably it. Not having time to think about being a failure at life meant finally feeling proud of myself for finding something that I was good at even if it was just waitressing. You know, actually I would go as far as saying that I was the best at it.

I always kept my section running as smoothly as possible and customers rarely had to ask for anything since I was great at anticipating what they needed. I was also a natural team player and even helped out other sections when I could. And not just because we were *supposed* to split tips since most didn't put much in the jar anyway. I just liked seeing happy customers and knowing that I'd played a part in making somebody's day.

And once I was eventually in charge of everything the experience would only get better. Not only would I revamp the uniforms, but I would also find some great cooks to whip up all those old family recipes and put Mae's name right back out front where it belonged.

"Alright now come meet Wendy," I heard Lena say right when I'd finally made time for a quick bathroom break. I sighed then turned to see that she was still training Blonde Fro so I knew I'd been right about Red Locs being the one to quit.

"Fuck these other bitches in here, but be nice to her and tip out. She don't have no kids or a man and sis barely leaves the house so she's always your first stop if you need somebody to cover your shift."

I couldn't help but laugh to myself at how my lack of a social life had become part of the new hire training, but I also cringed a little because even though Lena didn't mean any harm my life was exactly as boring and predictable as she'd described it.

Since I had been back in Chicago I'd felt the need to save as much as I could. A part of it genuinely was because I never wanted to find myself in a situation where I didn't have money again. But a bigger part was that I felt like I didn't deserve to have fun until I finally got myself and my life together for good. So until that day came I would remain at home lost in a good book or bingeing *The Real Housewives of Everywhere* using the diner's spotty Wi-Fi.

We were deep into March then, but it still felt like December since spring was taking her sweet time coming through. When I felt a biting chill suddenly hit my bare legs I looked towards the entrance to see a man holding the blood red doors for a group of women slowly coming in. Despite the slightly snowy ground outside they were in open-toed heels and being careful not to slip on any ice.

I immediately knew that the man wasn't with the younger women because they were dressed up for a night on the town while he looked out of place in a nice business suit at this hour. I was trying to see where we could possibly squeeze the newcomers in when somebody suddenly grabbed my wrist to get my attention. My reflexes caused me to instantly snatch away and I felt justified when I saw who the culprit was.

His name was Damion and he'd left his number on a napkin the last time he was in, but I had thrown it away with the rest of his trash then.

"Sorry. Did I scare you?"

Of course you did.

"No. You're fine," I said through a fake, perky smile as I glanced down at his clean plate. "You want your check or do you have enough room for dessert?"

I didn't really care, but this was a part of the job. Upselling meant a bigger bill which could ultimately result in a bigger tip.

"Only if I can order a slice of *you* to go, Wendy," he joked and I playfully laughed along even though I was internally disgusted.

Corniness aside he wasn't a bad looking guy at all, but being hit on at work was just not the move that men thought it was. On the street I could've kept walking and ignored him, but here my money depended on keeping him happy so I had to keep that in mind while letting him down.

"That's sweet, but the best I can do tonight is pie or cobbler," I said as I avoided eye contact then pointed to the daily dessert specials on the counter. From my peripheral I could see that his demeanor changed when he realized I wasn't receiving him the way he'd wanted me to.

"Just the check then," he said bitterly then I sped off to get it before he was even done speaking so I could at least seat the guy by the door in his spot. By the time I'd brought it back though Lena had already cleared a counter seat for him and a table for the women.

"Enjoy the rest of your night," I told Damion as I attempted to leave his check on the counter, but he insisted on grabbing my arm before I got too far away.

"Okay please don't touch me again," I said trying to control my tone and volume even though he was asking for me to misplace my last bit of *give a fuck*.

"You didn't call. Is there a reason for that?" he asked as if I owed him an explanation.

I kept my face as even as possible as I reminded him of our unofficial motto—You might be sweet, you might give head, but Jimmy's girls don't get their meat where they get their bread.

"We're not supposed to do that."

"Really? I didn't get that vibe here. Seems like just about anything goes," he said looking over at a booth where one of the other waitresses was laughing and practically sitting on a man's lap.

"Yeah well unlike some people I prefer to follow the rules," I retorted trying to give him one last chance to back off before he completely embarrassed himself. He did not take it.

"You know…you're really not even bad enough to be acting so stuck up. I'm a nice guy and I would've treated you good, but you just missed out," he spat finally releasing his entitled inner sourpuss with no shame.

I didn't even bother responding to his childish outburst and instead stuck to Jimmy's scripted valediction, "You have a great evening and we hope to see you again soon." And with that I went back to checking on my other tables.

I actually hoped that I never did see him in here again, but even if he decided to return I was at least grateful that he wouldn't be in my section. I knew his type all too well. They would come in a few times and leave huge tips trying to make a good impression then pounce once they felt comfortable.

It felt predatory or like grooming since even the "nice guys" like him knew that asking us out their first time in would almost guarantee being rejected. But if they were patient and became a regular, they figured they might be able to eventually weasel their way in.

It never worked with me.

I had personally seen how many of the girls stayed in unnecessary and very avoidable drama trying to sneakily date the customers, but I believed in service with a smile not a side of sex.

This was not *Coyote Ugly* and we were there to look cute and wait tables not entertain them.

"How much did he leave you this time?" Lena asked once Damion was eventually out of the door. I had seen her listening in on our conversation, hoping that I would finally go off like she did sometimes, but I knew he wasn't worth raising my pressure or getting lectured by Jimmy about not satisfying the customers.

"Two funky ass dollars?" she exclaimed after I held them up for her to see, but it didn't bother me since I was surprised that he had bothered leaving anything at all after our exchange.

On principle I was always grateful for every penny left for me because I knew that some people honestly didn't have it to give. But on the other hand I couldn't ignore the fact that the people who worked me the hardest or ordered the most usually left the least.

"She might get more than ten percent if she let loose every now and then," a familiar male voice said from the table behind me.

Lena and I both turned at the same time to see yet another obnoxious guy that had tried the same tricks on just about every waitress in here. But with a face and attitude like his, he could've tipped *one thousand percent* and it still wouldn't have been enough to get a date.

"Thank you for your suggestion, sir, but here at Jimmy's we appreciate all tips the same, big and small," I said purposely letting my eyes fall to the baby carrot energy coming from below his belt. "You have a great evening and we hope to see you again soon."

Lena laughed at his face dropping then followed me to the back because now I really did have to use the restroom. She fixed her hair and makeup while I peed and complained for the umpteenth time about how some of these customers really had us fucked up.

The night finally began to wind down after the game was over and the highlights had been highlighted, but we pretty much cleared out around eleven when a fight almost broke out. Jimmy, who only came out of his office for emergencies, managed to get it under control before it got out of hand, but every native Chicagoan knew to immediately vacate any premises when younger guys started acting up.

So nobody was surprised to see that the few remaining tables lacked melanin and I smiled to myself about them being so oblivious just because we were close to downtown. For the most part things were pretty chill on the northwestish side of the city, but they could and sometimes did get poppin' over here too.

One by one the *Friends* reunion cast all poured out and I thought I was finally free to go until Lena came from the back with her baby fur coat and boots on. I could have sworn I'd seen her leave with the other waitresses a little while ago, but apparently she'd just been in the bathroom on her phone the whole time.

"Wendy, my baby's waiting up for me. Cover my last booth, pleeease," she whined out to my surprise because I didn't think there was anybody else in there with us except for Jimmy in his office and one cook.

My eyes scoured her section only to land on that one guy in the business suit from before. I assumed the counter's stool must've gotten uncomfortable for his long legs because he had helped himself to an empty booth at some point during the night.

"Does it look like I care about you and Greg being nasty tonight?" I asked as I playfully rolled my eyes because I was sure anybody with their own could see how exhausted I already looked.

"C'mon. You're already at home, but I still gotta drive all the way out south and I'm getting sleepy," she exaggerated with a long yawn because I knew she would be doing backflips on her man the second she got home. I still fell for it and agreed though because I didn't want her leaving out on her own any later anyway.

"Thank you! Okay he only had two coffees all night, but I can tell he's got big tip energy so just be patient," she said loud enough for him to hear, but a glance in his direction proved that he couldn't care less about our conversation. His eyes were still glued to the TV screen how they had been for hours.

"What's his name?" I asked since knowing and using a customer's name was a great way to make them feel special and keep them coming back. She looked through her server's pouch for it for a few seconds before finally giving up.

"It was Kel something. Just call him Kel," she said waving me off as she scurried out in a hurry like I would change my mind.

After watching Lena pull off into the night, I kept myself busy by cleaning up after the cleanup crew since they were notorious for missing obvious stuff like the crumbs around the cake stands on the counter. It was a miracle that we didn't have problems with pests, but then again Jimmy kept some country concoction on hand sent up from our cousins in Mississippi.

Finally after every table was bussed, the tips were split, the bathrooms were cleaned and the grill was off, I just knew this guy would be ready to go, but he was still sitting there watching an infomercial at nearly midnight. Even Jimmy had fallen asleep on the couch in his office since no matter how late he had to be there, he would stay and count then recount the earnings from the day.

In all of that time I hadn't even bothered asking if he needed more coffee because he'd barely touched the one in front of him. I knew some people just liked killing time or avoiding going home for as long as possible though. Every now and then we did have problems with men waiting around until some of us clocked out, but Jimmy had a big, dense wooden bat for times like that.

He didn't give me a negative vibe though so when my feet had finally had enough, I loudly cleared my throat from behind the counter then attempted to politely tell him that while he didn't have to go home, he did have to get the hell up out of here.

"Hey if you're not going to order anything else could I give you the check? I don't mean to be rude, but I can't leave until you do and my feet are really killing me today."

Quickly tearing his eyes from the screen, he looked around confused like he didn't know where he was or maybe it was just because he'd been expecting Lena instead of me. He immediately sat up from his slouched position before speaking.

"Sorry about that. I must have lost track of time. What's the damage?" he asked before checking his watch for the time then reaching inside of his pocket for his wallet.

"Uh…the register's already been counted so don't worry about it," I said after checking to make sure Jimmy couldn't hear me because he was like a real life Mr. Krabs around here sometimes.

"Thanks. I really didn't mean to make you stay so late though," he said through a tired yawn as he put some cash on the table anyway. "Do you mind if I use the bathroom before I go?"

"Well the one for customers has already been cleaned and locked, but you can just go around through the kitchen and use the employee's. If Pedro stops you just say I sent you."

Usually I only did stuff like that for regular customers, but I took pity on the guy since he seemed to be having a bad enough day which didn't need to end with him having to pee outside in the cold. And since Chicago PD loved to cruise around this neighborhood at night to make a *certain* demographic feel safe now, I knew he didn't need those problems and I had definitely seen people taken in for less.

When he thanked me again I noticed that he didn't have any particular regional dialect, but I instantly knew he couldn't have been from around here because he'd left his belongings at the table while he went to use the bathroom. If I was a different kind of person I was sure I could have slipped something out without him even noticing, but lucky for him I preferred to make my money the honest way.

A few minutes later he gave me an appreciative nod on his way back out then finally gathered his things to go. One last polite but mostly sad smile and he was almost out of the door.

Til this day I still didn't know what compelled me to say something to him because I was never one of those servers who acted like a part-time counselor. I liked getting people fed then quickly getting them out of my hair, but with him I felt like I had to make sure he knew that his storm would be out of rain before he knew it.

"It'll be okay, you know?" I said pretty evenly even though I had tried to slip some sympathy in there. Apparently it was just enough for him to close the door and walk back towards me.

"Excuse me?" he asked even though I knew he'd heard me loud and clear.

This is why you should mind your business more.

"Um…whatever it is that you're worrying about. I'm sure it'll be okay."

"What makes you think I'm worrying about something?"

"Maybe because you're probably the saddest person I've ever seen in here. And that's saying something since *I* have to come every day."

That garnered a small but genuine smile out of him and two of the deepest dimples imaginable revealed themselves from just beneath his neatly trimmed facial hair. I had such an irrational weakness for those little indentations so of course that led me to finally taking the rest of him into consideration.

He was practically the prototype for tallish, dark and handsome, but it was all for naught though because a full once-over let me know that his cufflinks alone could buy this place in the blink of an eye. A woman like me was definitely not on his romantic radar for anything other than a good time so I immediately tucked my attraction away then waited for him to leave for good.

He remained in the same spot for a few seconds too long though before speaking again.

"You have a safe ride home?"

"I am home," I said pointing towards the ceiling before realizing that I had just foolishly let a strange man know where I lived.

"That must be convenient."

"Yeah I suppose it's a gift, but it can definitely be a curse when people don't show up for work. That's actually why I'm here now," I said through a yawn of my own as I walked over to lock the door after him.

"So you usually work mornings then?" he asked curiously and I hesitantly nodded because I had just basically laid out my schedule for him too.

"Uh yeah sometimes, but I do switch things up from time to time," I said trying to sound vague even though I was here faithfully from sunrise to sunset every day except for Sunday.

"Will you be here tomorrow morning?" he asked forwardly though I didn't detect any flirtation in his tone. It was still just general curiosity. That's when I decided that he was more than likely harmless so I was free to respond honestly.

"Bright and early."

"Alright I guess I'll see you tomorrow then. And maybe I'll actually try some food instead of just wasting my coffee again," he joked and lucky for him I had one more forced smile in me.

"Yeah you have a good one," I said before locking up and watching him get into a surprisingly sensible black car down the block.

Free at last!

I almost ran to get my things from the back, but I stopped in my tracks when I saw a crisp hundred dollar bill on the table he'd just been sitting at. Lena had literally been right on the money about his big tip energy, but I suddenly got a funny feeling about it since he didn't seem like he was completely paying attention when he'd left it.

Now obviously he looked like money and could probably spare it, but just because he had it like that didn't mean he intended to give it to me. That kind of thing did happen to other girls every now and then too and it was always awkward so I decided to keep it in my bag overnight to be sure.

After telling Pedro that he could go, I knocked on Jimmy's open door so he could finally head home to Paula too.

"Is he gone?" he asked stretching out on the worn out brown couch that was probably older than I was.

"Yep. See you in the morning. I'm going up."

"Not before you give me my five dollars and twenty cents for his two decaf coffees," he said with an amused cackle that led to him coughing a little. "This ain't no damn soup kitchen. This a business and you need to learn that while you tryna play boss around here, Lil' Bit."

I just sighed and gave him a ten from my tips and predictably his cheap ass pretended not to have any change. But as much as I disliked his penny-pinching ways, he did have a point…sometimes.

Jimmy was famously frugal and did not believe in comping meals or giving out free food. It was one of those things we were known for, right next to the fluffy flapjacks and short skirts. If there wasn't a severed finger next to your French toast then you had to pay for it. And if you didn't like his policy then he would tell you that his name was on the sign outside and not to come back.

But the funniest thing was that no matter how rude he was to people they *always* came back. He would say it was because the food was actually just that good, but I had other theories and wished that I could use him as a case study in the business class I planned on taking in the summer.

By the time my head finally hit my pillow I just knew that I would be fast asleep, but instead I rolled around for a while thinking about everything under the sun. Shutting off my brain at night had always seemed to be just as impossible as those nasty Impossible burgers we'd been pushing in the diner for months now.

I aimlessly scrolled on social media for a while and "loved" plenty of pictures that made me feel inadequate. They were of people I hadn't seen in years who probably wouldn't care if I double-tapped or not, but I did it anyway because, you know, it was the right thing to do to prove I wasn't a hater. And I actually wasn't. I just couldn't wait for the day that I could finally get on Facebook and not feel like such a loser anymore too.

When my eyes eventually got too heavy to keep open, I made myself put the phone down because I had another long day ahead of me tomorrow and then one more after that. Usually I would groan when I realized it wasn't time for my one day off yet, but for some strange reason I found myself kind of looking forward to work in the morning and that hadn't happened to me since…well ever.

I was too tired to even try to decode my fluctuating emotions though. Instead I drifted off to the sound of my fan and a fleeting thought about potentially doing something special for myself with that hundred dollar bill because I had earned it.

EARLY BIRD SPECIAL
MARCH 22ND

2

I never wore makeup to work. Okay scratch that. I moisturized, I used under eye concealer and I wore a shade of lipstick that matched my natural lip color so in the vast world of makeup *I never wore makeup to work.*

And don't get me wrong. I liked makeup and I could watch tutorials for hours without coming up for air, but every other day it seemed like there was some new step added and I could never keep up. That plus the fact that coming to work in a full face just wasn't practical for me especially during summer months because the AC was always breaking down.

But anyway that day I woke up a few minutes earlier than usual feeling refreshed and wanting to put in a little effort for a change. It was still dark out so the sun was barely peeking through my windows, but already I'd decided that I would have a good day.

I sat at the vanity that I'd gotten half off at Target then tried for all of ten minutes before giving up. My liquid foundation had somehow gotten separated since the last time I'd used it and the drugstore blush was making me feel like Pennywise so I wiped it all off.

I wouldn't let that ruin my good mood though so I decided to instead do something different with my hair. I usually kept it in a simple high puff to keep it equally out of my face and out of folks' food, but today I opted for not one but *two* afro puffs to really make a statement.

They were super cute too and just when I'd thought that a winged eye, which I couldn't apply to save my life, would go perfect with the look there was a knock on my door. I knew it could only be Lena coming to use the bathroom so I didn't bother putting on my robe.

She hated how small the ladies' room was in the diner and often told me it needed to be the first thing to remodel once I took over. I knew it would be forever and a day before that happened, but just the fact that she believed in me and spoke like everything was already mine felt nice. Especially since the original plan was for us to go halfsies and buy it together, but she had an addiction to retail that she couldn't kick and never saved much.

I had barely said *Good Morning* before she rushed passed me and dropped her stuff in my doorway. I just shook my head and thanked God that even though we shared a passing resemblance that I didn't get the weak bladder gene that she shared with the other women in the family. When she finally emerged now calm and collected she was met with all of my makeup laid out for her.

"Hey my favorite cousin," I began which let her know I was up to something. "Please do my makeup. Nothing dramatic. Just cute. You owe me from last night," I added just in case she thought about saying no.

"What's the occasion?" she asked instead as she put her things down then emptied her bag on my bed to use some of her high end products on me too.

"No reason. I just felt like doing something different today," I lied because in the back of my mind just knowing that the man from last night would be in again at some point made me want to look more put together than I'd looked at the end of my double shift.

"You sure it don't have nothing to do with that chump with chump change from last night?" she asked reminding me of how Damion had implied I wasn't pretty enough to reject him.

That definitely wasn't it though because in general I thought of myself as cute, really cute sometimes. But then again cute quickly got lost in the sea of sexy that was the serving staff at Jimmy's. We had a waitress in every shape, size and shade and they were all beyond gorgeous and done up every shift.

"Nope. I forgot all about that until now," I said honestly because the man's sad eyes were what was actually stuck in my head. I just couldn't figure out why though because having sympathy for a man, let alone a well-off man was so not me.

And I mean I knew money wasn't everything, but it definitely could've solved about ninety-nine of my problems right about then.

"Ooh we're twinning today. You look just like me," she said after I'd gotten fully dressed.

We took the last few minutes before it was time to head down to the diner to pose side by side in front of my floor length mirror. I liked almost all of the pictures we took, but standing next to her once again had me wishing that I was blessed with a little more up top and a lot more behind me.

Lena and a good amount of the other waitresses were thicker than the oatmeal we served which left me feeling like I didn't measure up some days. But I quickly put that behind me because again I'd decided that today I was Ice Cube and I would have a good day.

No sooner than I had clocked in and washed my hands, I heard the bell above the door ring out indicating that the first customer of the day had come in. It was barely seven so I was positive that it couldn't be *him* just yet, but still I found myself looking out through the server's window to make sure.

To my surprise it indeed was *Tallish, Dark and Handsome* in the flesh and he was wearing the hell out of another dark suit. Oblivious to me watching him, he took a seat in Lena's section again since the place was empty and he was free to sit exactly where he'd been the night before.

"Back so soon?" Lena greeted him warmly as she placed a menu in his hands. "Can I get you coffee, tea, fresh juice or water to start?"

"Hey actually I was looking for Wendy. Is she here yet?" TDH asked and before I knew it I'd knocked over one of those big stainless steel bowls that the cooks used for the flapjack and waffle batter.

Real smooth Wendy.

Luckily there was a wall separating him from seeing my clumsiness, but one of the cooks loudly called me by name and told me to be careful.

"It sounds like Wendy is busy making a ruckus right now. Are you sure that I can't get you anything?"

"Thanks, but I don't mind waiting on her," he said politely right as I came out of the kitchen, doing my best to pretend like I didn't see him.

I couldn't keep it up for long though because I felt his eyes on me which of course forced me to look in his direction. When our eyes synced he smiled big then waved over at me like we were more familiar than we actually were.

"Mm hm. I bet he don't mind waiting on you," Lena said before giving me a sneaky smile over her shoulder when we passed by each other.

He put the menu down as I approached and for a split second there I almost got worried, wondering how he had caught my name because I didn't remember throwing it to him. Then I relaxed and felt silly when I realized that it was literally handstitched on the left side of all my uniforms.

"Hey. Told you I'd be back."

"That you did. Can I get you some coffee to start?" I asked unintentionally speaking to him at a much softer volume for some reason.

I didn't know why I was acting like I had never talked to an attractive man before, but I guess it was because he looked even better and less melancholy with the sun shining in on his wide smile. Still I kept my eyes on my pen and pad even though I only really used it for complicated orders.

"Yeah. Decaf. Two sugars. One cream."

"Two sugars, one cream coming right up."

Lena was already back behind the counter so she waited while I warmed his cup then poured it for me. Of course she wasn't just trying to be helpful though. From the way she looked me over I could tell that she'd finally clocked the reason for the extra pep in my step and wanted to tease me about it.

"So that's why you were primping, huh?"

"Primping? Who primped?" I denied sounding completely unconvincing since I had already been caught glancing at my reflection in the mirrors in the back.

"You primped, bitch. And I do not blame you at all because Mr. Kel is looking mighty scrumptious over there," she said shamelessly checking him out, but fortunately he was out of earshot and still looking over the menu.

"Please stop looking at him like that," I begged her before he got wind that he was the latest hot topic in here.

"Ooh look at you, already acting territorial over your man. I know that's right!" she laughed out at me before something juicier came to mind. "So what's tea? What you did to that man after I left for him to be back up in here already and asking for you by name?"

"Nothing. We just talked for a minute then he left," I said then swiftly walked away before she could ask any more questions.

"Ready to order?" I asked him as I placed the coffee in the middle of the table to make sure he didn't spill it with the oversized and overwhelming menu. It was super repetitive though and it felt like we used the same five ingredients to make a million of the same thing with a different name.

"Uh I don't know. What do you usually get?" he asked before closing it again to give me his full attention.

"Oh I never eat here," I blurted out before I realized how bad it sounded. "No, the food is fine and always freshly made, but smelling it all day kind of kills my appetite for it," I said trying to clean it up, but the lines in his forehead and the adorable expression he wore didn't seem to believe me.

"We're famous for our flapjacks. How about I bring you out a stack to start?" I suggested while I held back a grin.

"Flapjacks it is then," he agreed before handing the menu back over.

"Alright that's flapjacks for...Kel," I said remembering what Lena had just called him as I scribbled on my pad.

"No. No. No. It's Kellen. **Never** Kel," he said like there was a story there, but I didn't bother prying.

"Okay. Kellen *never Kel*. Anything else?"

"Just another coffee," he said right as he was getting started on the first probably because our cups were so small.

"Got it." I turned to walk away, but I suddenly had a hunch and almost felt compelled to be right about it. "Keith and Helen, right?" I asked before watching his brows wrinkle in confusion. "Your parents' names."

"Ohhh. No, but you were close. *Kenneth* and Helen," he corrected with another smile. "How did you know?"

"Because I'm a victim of name combiner parents too," I told him as I tapped my stitched nametag with my pen. "I go by Wendy, but it's actually Wendella."

Wendella Elaine Bell to be exact, but he didn't need to know all of that...yet.

"That's one I haven't heard before. Let me guess...Wendell and..." he began before I finished it off for him because it was super obvious.

"Wendell and Ella." The moment my parents' names left my lips a strange feeling came over me because it hadn't dawned on me just how long it'd been since I'd last said them out loud.

"Hey! You didn't even give me a chance. That would've been my guess too," he playfully pouted.

"I'm sure it would've been," I teased him back. "Now let me go put this order in and grab your coffee. I'll be right back."

While I was warming Kellen's second cup to keep the coffee hot longer, one of the early bird regulars came stomping in like he owned the place. He was an ornery old Italian man that literally got the same thing every time he came in so I didn't even bother taking his order. I just greeted him then let him know it'd be out soon.

As I sat the cup down in front of Kellen, I suddenly remembered the hundred dollar bill in my pouch.

"Oh before I forget," I began as I reached in then sat it on the table, "I think you meant to give me a ten last night. Not this."

He took his time finishing off his first coffee before looking in his wallet to check. I nosily peeked to see if there were any pictures of kids or a wife, but all I saw was cash, a debit and a few business cards.

"Oh yeah I did actually, but do you always go around trying to return tips?" he asked sounding amused at me.

"No since a twenty is usually as good as it gets in here for me," I joked until he handed the money back.

"I guess that means you should keep it then. Glad I could be your first," he said with no humor this time so I knew he was serious.

"Oh no. It was an honest mistake. Here, take it."

I tried forcing him to accept it back, but he outright refused then playfully went back to drinking his coffee like I wasn't there. From the corner of my eye I saw Lena and two other waitresses heading into Jimmy's office and I remembered that it was payday so I followed after them.

I really didn't know why he bothered wasting all those trees on the pennies he paid us weekly, I thought as I looked over my ten dollar check.

I had done more than a few doubles the last couple weeks, but taxes just seemed to eat up what little extra I was supposed to make. I should have done like other girls and not claimed some of my cash tips, but I was always afraid of being audited or worse being shit out of luck when I would eventually need proof of income to buy the diner.

"Jimmy, how am I supposed to make ends meet when you keep paying us in grease and pit stains?" one of the newer girls complained.

"Maybe that's because I want you to come retire to Florida with me," he said with no shame even though Lena and I were standing there.

"In your geriatric dreams," she cracked then immediately left before he could react.

I saw his frown though and laughed to myself because he really thought somebody could want his old bony behind even as a sugar daddy. But just the mention of him retiring had me daydreaming about how different things would be when I took over.

For starters there would be no more rowdy men and sports nights because this place had the potential to be a real brunch hotspot if we tried to attract a younger Black female crowd instead. I wanted it to have a more upscale feel and I imagined bougie *and* boozy brunches with unlimited mimosas and rich, childless auntie laughter.

The vintage pink and green theme and the black and white checkerboard floors could even stay, but we definitely needed a jukebox that actually played music since apparently the one we currently had hadn't worked since the eighties. It was pointless to even suggest these things to Jimmy though since his only goal was to suck as much money as possible out of this place without having to spend any.

"Hey Powerpuff," I heard Carl, the older customer impatiently call out to me.

I knew from his tone that something must've been wrong with his meal, but then again the man's favorite pastime seemed to be complaining or trying to eat for free. He barely tipped us as is and used his fixed income as an excuse, but homeboy stayed in here for breakfast, lunch and dinner some days so I knew it was just a front for plain old cheapness.

I immediately checked to see what could be missing from his plate, but as it turned out it was the whole thing since he didn't even have it yet. Now I could've sworn I'd just given it to him, but the only plate under the heat lamps was a simple order of flapjacks.

That's when I realized what I'd done. In a rare case of server-brain for me, I'd given Carl's Denver omelet, home fries and grapefruit to Kellen. I looked over to find him eating it while looking at something on his phone. He definitely had the wrong food, but he seemed to be enjoying it because the big plate was already nearly empty.

I quickly explained to Carl what'd happened then instinctively went into apology mode, but he had to have woken up on the wrong side of the bed because even telling him that I would personally comp the meal for the wait didn't seem to satisfy him.

In general I had much more patience for my early customers because usually I didn't like having to be up so early either, but it seemed like he was deciding to tap-dance on my last nerve today just for the hell of it.

"How hard is it to remember the right table when there's only two?" he asked raising his voice even though I had remained calm during his pointless tirade. And not to mention that I literally could've had a new order out by that point if he hadn't still been going off.

You'll be dead by the end of my shift if you keep cutting up like this, old man.

"You're absolutely right, sir and if you'll just try to sit tight for a little longer I'll get a fresh order right out to you," I said trying to inch away, but he just kept throwing more insults my way.

"Yeah you do that. And might I add, maybe if you spent more time using your head instead of worrying about your cutesy hair weaves and whatnot, you might be able to do your very easy job correctly," he spat reminding me of the candidate that he'd most likely voted for in the last election.

And see no matter how insulting an exchange got I swore that I would never ever tamper with somebody's food as revenge, but customers like him definitely made me understand why other servers did.

And despite me brushing it off, I guess that last comment had been just enough for Kellen to finally step in because without turning his back or even raising his voice he got Carl together on my behalf.

"Hey my guy. Stop and think real hard about what you say to her next. Or better yet let me tell you what you're going to say. 'I apologize for insulting you and your beautiful *natural* hair and I promise it'll never happen again'," he said before glancing back at me to see my reaction, but Carl responding got my attention first.

"Oh yeah? And what are you gonna do about it if I don't, tough guy?" Carl challenged.

"Look if you're not happy with the service here, there's a McDonald's right up the street. Why don't you go grab something from there because after I take this last bite of your food I'm not gonna be so helpful with directions then," Kellen responded with a tad bit extra bass in his voice.

"Is that a threat?" Carl asked, but that time he didn't get an answer. Kellen just let his fork hit the plate and apparently that was all it took for Carl to huff and puff about *you people* then get back into his coat in record time.

And I swore that little limp he always had was even gone as he hurried back out into the cold. I wish I could've recorded it to show Lena because I knew she wouldn't believe me when I told her.

"Thanks. You have no idea how bad I want to tell these people to just relax sometimes. But why didn't you say anything about your food?"

"My fault. I thought you were just recommending something else since I didn't know what I wanted. And that guy might be a little racist, but he does have good taste," he said before finally finishing off his last bite.

"You think you can keep your head out of the clouds long enough to remember this for me tomorrow?" he asked casually before I realized it meant he must have been watching me while I was daydreaming.

"I'll see what I can do, but I'm not making any promises. And do you still want those flapjacks to go then?"

"Actually I'm pretty stuffed, but you know what? Give me a few more orders. I can give them to my team and pretend like I was being thoughtful for once," he said finally pulling a genuine smile out of me.

"You have a work team? What do you do?" I asked curiously because I had been dying to know anyway. The suits said lawyer, but he didn't seem sleep deprived or super serious like the others we had in sometimes.

"I run a 3D printing company not too far from here."

"Now that's one *I* haven't heard before. How'd you get into that?"

"It's a long boring story, but maybe I'll tell you one day when you need to be put to sleep," he joked, but for some reason something tingled in me at the thought of falling asleep near him.

And this time when I brought over his check he was definitely not distracted since he left the exact dollar amount and change for his meal then put *another* hundred dollar bill on the table, the same as he'd done the night before.

"Thanks again for what you said to me last night. I think I really needed to hear that."

"You're welcome and thank you too, but we're actually not supposed to take direct tips. You have to put it in the jar," I told him then stepped aside so he could see it on the counter behind me.

I almost detected a hint of a blush in his brown cheeks as he read the small chalkboard sign next to it.

<u>Just put the tip in. You know you want to.</u>

"You have to split that with everybody, right? Even the cooks?" he asked curiously before I nodded. "Then no. This is just for you, Wendy," he said while making sure no one was watching as he slyly put his tip into the pocket of my skirt.

A different type of man would have used the opportunity to *accidentally* graze my thigh, but he seemed to be just as deliberate with the placement of his hands as he was with his money and he kept them to himself.

I guess I must've spaced out for a second because I was still stupidly standing in his way when he stood to his feet. He didn't seem to mind though as he smiled down at my ditzy behind then squeezed by me.

"See you tomorrow," he said on his way out and I couldn't even describe just how quickly those words were becoming favorites of mine.

ORDER UP
MARCH 28TH

3

I had never really been an omelet kind of girl myself, but Kellen never Kel must've *really* enjoyed Carl's the week before because since then he'd been back in every day to get the exact same thing. He made sure to always be one of the first customers too, giving us ample time for a few jokes and just general lighthearted conversation.

Sometimes he even stopped by for lunch too which got pretty hectic around here, but no matter how busy my section was he would always insist on waiting around for me. According to Lena it wasn't the food that he was coming back for, but in spite of the obvious I couldn't say for sure that I agreed.

I mean for one he didn't seem very shy at all. He made then held eye contact with me whenever he spoke and he never once hesitated or stumbled over his words. He was the definition of confident and of course he had every right to be since there was no way that man didn't know how attractive he was. So basically I had no valid reason to believe that he wouldn't have made a move already…if he wanted to make a move.

I tried like hell to blame it on the fact that I could only keep up the extra makeup shtick for a few days. But I knew it couldn't have been that since I was back to being regular schmegular Wendy when one day out of the blue the conversation finally shifted from neutral to drive.

It started out innocently enough—*So how long have you worked here? Do you even actually like serving?*—You know, the usual until he went and pulled out the…

"You probably get hit on every day in here, don't you?" he asked trying to sound casual as I gathered his empty plate and coffee cups from the table. It was pretty early so not that many folks were in yet, but he still kept his voice at a private level.

"Um…sometimes, but it kinda comes with the territory. It's not even us really. It's this stupid uniform they're asking out," I said before realizing what was happening because he had previously lulled me into a false sense of security.

I'd accepted the fact that *this* scenario wasn't even a possibility with him so I hadn't bothered putting serious thought into what I would say. And it mattered because I couldn't just give *him* the same old tired excuses that I'd given other men. He was different.

"Yeah, I bet. Listen I know this is a longshot and stop me at any time if I'm wrong but talking to you this last week…I kinda got the feeling that we have a lot in common. And if you're not seeing anybody I want to take you out if that's alright with you?"

Even more than I was caught off guard that he'd finally asked, I was stunned that he thought *I* would reject somebody like *him*. And I mean he wasn't wrong since I immediately knew that I couldn't accept his invitation. It just wasn't for the reasons that he probably anticipated.

And calling the delay in my response an awkward silence would have been too kind since it took way too long for me to clear my throat and speak up. But still he just sat there patiently waiting for it.

It should be a crime to be this stupid.

"I don't really think that's a good idea. It's against the rules and--" I began, ready to list off all the reasons, but he cut me off to spare us both.

"Right. I understand. Sorry about that. I shouldn't have--" he began sounding genuinely apologetic before finally letting his eyes fall from mine. I felt bad too since he was taking rejection the way all men should have.

"No it's okay. I think you're really nice, Kellen. It's just…" I began but didn't exactly know where my words were headed so I sighed instead. "Let me get your check."

His order was literally always the same so I knew the total by heart now, but I still took a little longer than I needed ringing him up so that I could covertly watch him. There was no sudden hostility coming from his direction which was a welcome surprise, but I still anticipated a major reduction in that extra generous tip that he insisted on leaving for me every day.

I was wrong though because Lena, who had witnessed the whole exchange while shaking her head at me, signaled that he'd left his usual after I dropped off the check and scurried away before he had the chance to say anything else. And I didn't know why that made me feel like I had to explain myself to him, but it just did.

I guess it was because I knew he would be the type to never come back and even though I knew I couldn't date him that didn't mean I didn't want to ever see him again either. Before he could get too far out of the door I asked if he could wait for me outside.

"Don't tell me it's my lucky day and you changed your mind already?" he asked sarcastically as I stepped out of the diner and on to the well-salted sidewalk at a safe distance. I noted that he had conveniently managed to get the best parking spot right in front of the building that day as he leaned against his car.

"No. I just wanted to tell you that me turning you down…it's not about you. It's me," I told him being completely honest as I rubbed my cold arms, but his raised brows showed his disbelief. "No for real. I'm trying to focus on getting my shit together before I start dating again."

I used the word *again* pretty loosely there because it implied that I had ever really started. The stuff I'd done in high school and college barely counted as dating then let alone as an actual adult. And since getting to Chicago all I seemed to meet were men that had nothing to offer but unsatisfactory sex and emotional abuse so these days I passed on it altogether.

"About how long do you think that'll take?" he asked sounding impatient, but his adorable smile more than made up for it. "Not to rush you or anything, but you already seem 'together' to me."

"Well I'm not and I really don't know how long it'll be so you should probably just…you know divert this energy to somewhere it'll count."

He nodded in agreement but still slipped out of his long black trench coat then walked to drape it over my shivering shoulders. I hadn't been planning on staying out in the cold for much longer, but I guess since he finally had my undivided attention he wanted to plead his case more thoroughly…and closer.

We were the closest we had ever been, but even more than the heat from his coat swallowing me the warmth from his body in front of mine had me feeling pretty toasty too. And if his plan involved seducing me with his scent then it was working because the masculine teakwood in the air mixed with vanilla and maybe citrus was enough to make any woman reconsider.

I was sure that Lena and the other girls were inside neglecting tables watching me be a complete hypocrite out there, but I decided to instead focus on the pretty set of lips above me that still smelled like grapefruit.

"Look Wendy I know you get approached by sleazy dudes in here all the time and I'm not gonna lie and pretend like I'm not just like them because I am. I think you're beautiful and I like the way you look in your uniform too. In fact I hope you drop something every time I'm in here just so I can see you pick it up," he said sounding a little too candid which made me unintentionally blush and tug on the back of my skirt, wondering just how much he'd managed to see already.

"But the one difference between them and me is that I want to see everything else too. I want to know who you are outside of here, all the good, the bad, **everything**," he emphasized with conviction.

His earnest eyes were intense enough to make me tap out of our mutual gaze so I let mine fall down his tailored suit to our feet. If I didn't know any better, I would have thought I was in danger the way both of his long oxford shoes enveloped my little no name white sneakers. It was because he stood protectively over me and even though danger was nowhere to be found, I still found myself feeling really afraid of what was happening between us.

"Just trust me on this one, okay? You do not want to know anything about me, let alone the bad stuff," I said thinking about how just that morning I'd woken up in a pool of sweat caused from my anxiousness during sleep.

For the most part I was good at hiding my anxiety during the day, but I was always forced to feel it then when I was no longer in control. Just the thought of that warmed me even more and made me remember yet another reason I could never get involved with a normal, happy person like him.

They would never *get it* and I never wanted to feel like a burden in a relationship which was why I avoided them like the plague. He'd had one bad day a week ago but quickly got over it and was chipper ever since. Meanwhile dark clouds had been permanently camped out over my head since birth.

It would never work.

With a simple nod he acquiesced to my ominous warning and without speaking we acknowledged that the conversation was over so I returned his coat then went to head back inside.

"What if I said I didn't mind waiting?" he asked abruptly stopping me from reentering, but it wasn't until our eyes met again that he explained himself.

"I know from experience that you're an honest person Wendy because you're a waitress who returns tips. So however unlikely it is, I'm gonna take you at your word that *you're* the problem here and not me," he said making us both chuckle and it felt good to release some of the tension that we'd unexpectedly built up.

"Just work through whatever you have to then let me know when you're ready, alright?" he suggested like it was as easy as pie and for the first time in a long time I *really* wished that it was.

"That's not how it works, Kellen. There are no expiration dates on my issues so you'll just be wasting your time."

"Mm I think I'll be the judge of that. But on the other hand I don't have forever so Day One of *Wendy Gets Her Shit Together* officially starts tomorrow, alright. Make a list and check it twice," he teased as he unlocked his car then finally got into the driver's side.

"Kellen! No. We're not doing this," I laughed out because I couldn't believe that we were actually having this conversation and that this was his response to it.

"It's already done. I'll see you tomorrow," he said before correcting himself. "Wait. You don't work tomorrow so try not to miss me too much and I'll do the same, alright?" he instructed before pulling off into traffic and taking almost every shred of resolve and resistance that I had with him.

OVER EASY

APRIL 29TH

4

Over the next month or so Kellen Turner faithfully had his cute and firm butt seated in my section from Monday through Saturday for either breakfast or lunch and sometimes even dinner on nights when he knew I had that shift.

If he hadn't been just as funny as he was fine I would have considered him a bonafide stalker, but to his benefit he was funny and fine. And since he'd made his intentions for me crystal clear there was nothing left to do but wait him out.

Along with his cute butt, his big tips also kept coming and he basically let me know that there was no sense in arguing with it so I didn't even bother anymore. A part of me was still wary about accepting so much money from a man even though it was clear that it wasn't breaking the bank for him. I just put it all in my diner fund which because of him was already looking like it wasn't on life support anymore.

Meanwhile Lena decided to use the situation to earn a little extra cash for herself as well. She combined her competitiveness with her hopeless romantic side and had everybody placing bets on how long it would take me to finally give Kellen a chance. The thought of him finding out what they were up to in the kitchen at the end of every week mortified me but not more than the general sentiment amongst the other waitresses —Why her?

Not to mention everybody and their mother making it their business to let me know to hurry up and jump on it because a man like that wouldn't wait around for too long. They weren't exactly telling me anything that I didn't already know though and in fact I was actually hoping he wouldn't wait so that I could be let off the hook and not feel guilty about it.

I knew I wasn't exactly worth all the trouble or the tips he was going through, but at the same time I didn't want *him* to ever know that so it was best that the idea of us stayed just that…an idea.

Still I had come to expect and even get internally excited at the way his eyes lit up with a familiar warmth when he came in and saw me every day. It was nice knowing that little ol' Wendy had that kind of effect on somebody whether I planned on acting on it or not. And I really wasn't planning on it, but eventually I did get curious about him too.

Like who the hell was he and where did he come from and why did he just blow in like the wind that one night and never leave? *And why was he so damn fixated on me?*

When I'd looked him up online I saw that he was a much bigger deal than even I had initially picked up on in the home décor world. In an interview with *Forbes* he'd said that his 3D printing company was a way to merge his two loves, science and the woodworking he did as a kid with his late grandfather. I thought it was a sweet story, but after seeing the prices on just one of his end tables I knew exactly why it was being told in *Forbes* and how he could afford those fly blue suits and cufflinks.

More digital digging told me that his family wasn't new to money at all. He had been raised a little bit more than upper middle class up north in Lincoln Park but spent many years away after earning a mechanical engineering degree from MIT. That explained the hints of a Boston accent that came through every now and then on certain words. Like every time he asked…

"Still don't have it together yet?"

"Not yet."

"Then the wait continues…"

About once a week he had been playfully requesting a verbal progress report on how I was doing with working on my list. That night in particular it was late and I'd had a long day so when he asked I kept it real and shared that the majority of my work fell more on the mental side. I told him how I had gotten back into therapy not long after moving back, but I still struggled with changing the way I looked at things.

"But I'm thinking about shaking things up and getting a new therapist altogether. This one just keeps telling me to find something to do besides work and sleep. Apparently there's this thing called fun that's supposed to be all the rave these days," I said sarcastically because he was still in that phase where men actually listened and laughed at your jokes.

Plus his big dimpled smile was unmatched and I would say almost anything just to see it every now and then. If I could just swirl my tongue around inside of one...

"Fun, huh? Yeah I think I've heard of that. And actually I've been told that *I* can be a lot of fun. Just putting it out there again in case it's relevant to anybody you might know," he responded matching my tone and I really appreciated how even when he was obviously being flirtatious, he was still always respectful of the fact that I was at work.

From looking into his wild eyes so much I could tell that he had a dark side, but he never once got inappropriate with me. Even when I would catch him watching me *like that* sometimes, he was charming enough to flip it into something syrupy sweet.

"You look really pretty today, Wendy."
"I look the same as I always look, Kellen."
"That doesn't make it any less true."

But even with as patient as he claimed to be, I knew he was getting hot feet about how long the wait had already been when he finally inquired about the other things on my *Wendy Gets Her Shit Together* list.

"Wait you really have buying a restaurant on the list before you'll date me? You really don't want this to happen, do you?" he asked before we shared a hearty laugh, but his stopped first with a no sweat offer to buy it for me.

I laughed harder because he was clearly still playing around...until I really looked at him and realized that maybe he wasn't.

"Kellen, I'm not letting you buy me anything. Your tips are already helping out just fine."

"Yeah but you're gonna need much bigger tips if you're planning on taking over this place. No offense," he said as he took a more thorough look around.

"None taken. I know it's a fixer upper. Kinda reminds me of myself that way."

"Okay forget the therapist. We need to get you a new eye doctor because we cannot be looking at the same person."

"Well thank you, but I'm not just talking about the outside...even though I could definitely use a little work on the outside too." I mumbled out the latter half from under my breath as I started wiping the counters down, but his bigger hand being placed on top of mine quickly brought it and my negative thoughts to a stop.

"Where?" he asked in disbelief since he personally seemed pleased with everything that was in his line of sight.

I was thinking of something slick to say when I was suddenly summoned to a booth near the door. It was that rude guy Damion and a few of his friends so I hadn't exactly been in a rush to tend to their every need how I had done the rest of my section all night. In fact once I was cleared of everybody but them and Kellen, I'd spent all my time behind the counter laughing and updating him on the previous week's progress.

Damion had been back in a few times since our little run in before, but it was the first time that he and Kellen were both present at the same time. Aside from annoyed once-overs we hadn't made any contact with each other before I'd taken his order earlier, but there was a different energy in the air after the table had gotten a few rounds in them.

"Can I get you anything else? I'm about to give them their check then get ready to get up out of here," I told Kellen since he had already picked up on me avoiding those guys for a while.

"I'm alright. I'll wait for you to close up though," he said in the protective tone that I'd gotten used to hearing when he showed up for the tail end of my rare dinner shifts.

It was clear he saw himself as some kind of security for not just me but the other girls too since he had pulled out his stern voice whenever it was getting late and certain guys didn't want to accept defeat for the night.

To my surprise the table of clearly drunk and high guys just wanted their checks, all separate of course, and a few to-go boxes for their last round of our endless wings promotion. I didn't know where Jimmy got those humongous things every month, but folks from all over the city came in every Friday just for them.

They looked more pterodactyl then poultry though so I gave Kellen our regular wings when he'd ordered his. His appetite seemed to come and go some days though and he mostly picked over them and instead drank a bottle of water while we talked.

Now I didn't know what had happened behind my back from the time I left Damion's booth until I got to the kitchen, but I wasn't in there for a full five seconds before I heard loud commotion coming from the front of the diner. I was no firefighter so running towards danger was not in my job description, but I couldn't help myself when I heard Kellen's voice sounding more aggressive than I'd ever heard it before.

When I opened the swinging door he and Damion were nose to nose with Jimmy trying to split them up. Even without confirmation I knew it had something to do with me giving Kellen the attention that Damion previously requested from me so I did my part to deescalate the situation. Neither seemed too interested in what I had to say though so I physically got in front of Kellen since he had been pretending not to hear me from behind.

His eyes instantly softened when they lowered to meet mine and he backed down from the impending melee without another word. Things seemed to be calming down for a minute and everybody was going their separate ways until Jimmy clocked the guys trying to leave without paying their bill.

And of course Kellen's ego just couldn't let him pass up the opportunity to let them know not to worry about it. He offered to take care of their tab since he had just overheard them arguing over who had ordered what. And just like anybody else I could appreciate a little pettiness in moderation, but it really wasn't needed then as proven by Damion's lackeys actively getting involved against him at that point.

Jimmy and one of the line cooks hurried and helped me escort Mr. Turner to the back of the restaurant while the remaining staff let the other guys out of the front. By then Kellen's anger had passed just as quickly as it had come so he assured us he was fine to leave too, but I wasn't taking any chances with how things had just turned up so fast.

"No. Just stay here for a little while. For me. Please," I ordered as I grabbed his hand and brought him passed Jimmy's office to the rear stairs that led up to my apartment.

I knew Jimmy would finally be giving me the warning about keeping my *little boyfriends* in check in his place of business the same way he had done for other girls, but I wasn't worried about that at the moment. I just wanted to get Kellen to stay as long as possible in case those guys were waiting around for him to leave by himself. A fleeting thought that could prevent the scenario popped in my head when we took a seat on the hard brown stairs.

Surely nobody would be willing to wait him out all night so if he were to say stay over with me then…

Nope.

I instantly disregarded the idea since I would never be bold enough to even platonically suggest anything like that and I really didn't want to blur the lines any more than they already were. But apparently they were more bleary than I'd thought since he immediately leaned back on his elbows and looked up at my door.

"So this is where you live, huh?" he asked even though he clearly already knew the answer. I just gave him a knowing look as I folded my arms across my chest. "What, it's not like I'm trying to go up there. You asked me to stay for a minute so I was just making conversation."

"Oh I'm sure you were Kellen never Kel," I yawned out and made sure to cover my mouth since we were in such close quarters.

Both our arms and legs were forced to make contact with each other on the narrow stairs and he even had to put an arm on the stair behind me just to sit comfortably…at least that's why I had told myself he'd done it.

"I really was. And just so you know I didn't come back here to hide from them and I've never been scared of a fight. I would just rather spend more time with you than bruise my knuckles tonight," he said being silly and I smiled at him trying to act tough for me when he was obviously more suited for *GQ* than *Fight Club*.

"I wasn't thinking that at all. I was thinking that you really can't be doing this anymore. It's not your job to be our security. Jimmy can handle that."

"Yeah but he works hard so I gave him the night off," he said sarcastically until he saw that I wasn't amused. "What kind of man would I be if I didn't? I'm not just gonna sit there and let somebody disrespect any woman in my presence and especially not you."

"Disrespect me how though? What, they said something when I left?"

"Yeah and I'm not gonna repeat it so don't ask," he said decisively, but I wouldn't dare bother since the little bit of self-esteem I had was already hanging on by a thread.

It was probably something about me needing some more ass. And I did.

"I couldn't care less what they said about me. What I care about is Jimmy possibly banning my new favorite customer because he thinks he's in a Marvel movie," I told him matter-of-factly and saw his eyes sparkle when I called him my favorite.

"Funny. I had you pegged as a DC type of woman, but I guess I can't expect everybody to have good taste like me," he said casually insulting my preference in superheroes before asking for my favorite film in the franchise.

Usually I would've gotten into a little back-and-forth about that kind of thing, but I had to remind him that being there was about his safety not getting into cutesy first date debates.

"C'mon. Give me something. If you haven't noticed I'm not just gonna let a little thing like you not going out with me stop me from getting to know you."

Am I allowed to put stuff that's just for me on our wedding registry?

"No. You already know way more about me anyway so let's get to know you some." I flipped it on him because it gave me the perfect excuse to ask something that'd been in the back of my mind for weeks now. "Why were you so down that first night you came in?"

I knew I was more than likely asking about a really sensitive subject, but I just had to know the reason because he honestly seemed like a completely different person then. Aside from the thing with Damion, he was literally always all smiles and it was the only thing about him that didn't add up.

"It's a long story," he said after an even longer pause and a heavy sigh.

"You've said that a couple times now. Just give me the cliff notes," I pushed even though every road sign in my brain was telling me to yield because there was danger ahead.

"Another time." The hint of annoyance in his voice should have deterred me from preceding further, but it didn't. I knew I had pushed him too far though when he couldn't maintain eye contact anymore.

"Look Wendy, you've got your boundaries and I've got mine. Let's just drop it, alright? I'm gonna head out," he said before pulling his wallet out to pay for everything and as usual he didn't forget my tip in his count.

"Have a good night," he said distantly as he prepared to stand, but my words acted as an anchor and kept him seated.

"Funny. I had you pegged as a 'talk things out' kind of guy, but I guess you're a runner just like me," I said mocking his previous movie hot take.

I could have tried to hide my disappointment at his lack of a response, but in that instance I knew things had officially ran their course so there was no need for any filtering.

"Uh oh. Why do I feel like I'm in trouble now?" he joked as he looked over at me, but his killer smile did nothing but reiterate that he was capable of turning it on and off at will.

Because you are.

"Not trouble per se, but I really don't think we should do this anymore," I said getting straight to the point as I stood because I was finally feeling just as mentally exhausted as I had been physically.

"Do what? We haven't done anything," he said with knitted brows even though I knew he knew what I meant.

"Yeah but it's already too much. I told you I'm not ready yet and you shoving all of this money in my pockets every day isn't gonna make it happen any faster. It's actually just making me uncomfortable."

"Okay what amount would make you more comfortable then?" he asked like he expected me to have a figure in mind, but I didn't because it was deeper than that. Silence loomed over us until he realized it. "It's not the money, is it? It's me, right? I make you uncomfortable?"

I actually intended on answering that question with the nuance that it deserved and required to keep us on good terms, but then he started speaking again and I decided to shut up at the wrong time.

"That's the last thing I was trying to do so I guess I'll have to find a new spot or maybe even try cooking at home for once," he weakly chuckled out.

I could tell that I had offended him, but instead of externalizing it he decided to take my words at face value and remove himself. I appreciated the sentiment even though it wasn't exactly the solution I was thinking of.

"Kellen, you don't have to do that. You could just like…I don't know…let somebody else wait on you," I suggested even though the thought of seeing him with anybody else was not a welcome one. Thankfully he thought the same as he immediately vetoed it with a shake of his head.

"Part of the charm of this place was waiting on you to find time for me," he said as he finally put the money in my hand and held on for a second too soon. "Sorry about all of this."

He went to stand again and suddenly almost tipped over in my direction, but I caught him at the same time as he caught himself.

"Whoa, you okay?" I asked with hands on his chest and stomach.

His skin felt firm but loose if that made sense, but he stepped back so quickly that my grand opening to touching him was also the grand closing. It was the first time I noticed that even though he looked fit, there was a slight bloat to him like he was retaining water.

"Yeah. My bad. Just got a little lightheaded I guess."

"Are you sure you don't need me to walk you to your car at least?" I offered as a last ditch effort because I didn't know what else to say to him. I just knew I didn't want it to be good night forever even though it definitely felt like that's what it would be.

"Hey hey. I'm still a man, alright?" he said with a smile that didn't quite reach his eyes.

I had read about that kind of smile in dozens of books before, but seeing it in person was like a dagger to the chest knowing that I had been the one to cause his.

"Take care, Wendy. And not that you need it, but good luck with the rest of your list."

LUNCH BREAK
MAY 20TH
5

I had done it. I'd been rolling dice for weeks trying to get my *Get Rid of Kellen Free* card, but the second I actually landed on it I knew I wanted nothing more than to reset the board and start a new game.

Lena had never teased me for losing a regular customer before because she knew it was usually preceded by them doing something gross like asking for a handjob in the back alley or worse. But she'd seen firsthand that Kellen wasn't like that so for that reason alone she decided to remind me of him and the bill I was missing every time we counted out tips.

I definitely hadn't been saving anywhere near as much as I did during his short tenure, but even more than the money I just missed him. It had been too long since I was mutually interested in anybody and I couldn't even remember the last time I'd smiled that much. And even though I knew I still wasn't all the way ready for him, that didn't stop me from wanting to get that old thing back.

He had been gone for exactly three weeks when Lena finally convinced me that showing up to his company with his favorite lunch wouldn't look desperate on my part. It was obviously a lie from the pit of hell, but she'd told it and I was actually considering it because neither of us could come up with another route to reel him back in.

It was a good thing it'd taken her so long to hype me up to do it too because literally a few minutes after asking her what I would even say to him when I got there, in waltzed Mr. Turner in the flesh. I was surprised he could even finish his phone call the way his ears should have been ringing, but I was for sure left on mute as the battery Lena had just put in my back immediately lost its charge.

I tried to look busy organizing the already organized menus behind the counter as he waited to be seated since we were just about half full for lunch.

Box Braids, the newest and by far the bustiest addition to the wait staff, was on him fast and asked me to hand her a menu from my stack. But the thought of him staring at her breasts— whose authenticity Lena and I had been debating over for two days —left me feeling frozen and inadequate so I didn't know how she had gotten the one she gave to him.

"Hey Kellen. Long time no see," Lena said sounding breezy and friendly as he passed us and I had never wanted to melt into my body more than when he spoke back to her.

I couldn't even muster up a reaction so I just turned to check the coffee levels in case we needed to make more. Jimmy clearly hadn't hired

Box Braids for her ability to follow instructions because she had to have been the one not using our simple refill system.

I wouldn't be too hard on her though because she'd already overshared her life story the day before and it was rough enough without me adding to it because I was a jealous flat-chested bitch

"Now's your chance. Go get your man back before these bitches swarm him," she said at a lower volume, but it still wasn't quite the whisper that it should have been.

"Are you crazy? He literally just walked by without even speaking to me," I argued even though I had purposely avoided any direct contact with him as well.

"So? I wouldn't have spoken to your little ungrateful ass either after the way he was cashing you out," she said playfully. "But he's back now so that means he's willing to meet you halfway only the next play is on you. So go play ho!" she instructed as she nudged me in his general direction.

I slowly walked up to him from behind like I might actually do it, but I ultimately chickened out and decided to go check on my tables instead. I had to work hard to ignore Lena's back to back loud sighs as I went back into server mode.

Without being too obvious I watched Box Braids and Kellen as closely as I could. He was still a man, as he had so aptly reminded me the last time we saw each other, so he definitely took a gander at her twins, but it was a short and sweet glance before asking for coffee.

Her first mistake was putting a cold cup and saucer on the table, but her second mistake, not paying attention and accidentally over-pouring it, was the one that would cost even the best server their tip. Lucky for him she'd forgotten to keep the warmer button on too since he wouldn't have been able to remain calmly seated had it been hot.

"Oh my goodness! I am so sorry," she said in her little cute country twang before continuing to apologize like it was going out of style as she gave him more napkins for his lap. "It's only my second day."

I could tell that he was less than pleased at his now wet pant leg, but he still assured her that it wasn't that big of a deal especially since he was wearing black.

After quickly passing out my checks I approached his table to come to her rescue. More than I wanted to help him I wanted to help her because I could tell she thought she would be in trouble from the way Jimmy came out of his office to see what all the noise was about.

"I can take care of this, Box Br--I mean Jenna. You can go on break if you want," I told her sympathetically and watched as she hurried up and made her way back to the kitchen.

Stop staring at him! Just say hi.

"Hey Kellen. How are you?" I asked trying to sound as easy-going as Lena, but I obviously hadn't inherited that gene like she did.

"Could be better. Do you finally see why I prefer to just wait on you?" he asked sarcastically as he pointed to his lap, but I could tell that overall he wasn't too upset at the spill since it had gotten my attention.

"Yeah good thing the coffee wasn't hot either or Jimmy would've had to put your name out front after you finished suing him," I joked and finally relaxed some when I saw that familiar smile spread across his face like the butter on our toast.

"Only if you would've let me give it to you," he said before leaning in so only I could hear him. "And just to be clear, I really wasn't planning on bothering you at all today, Wendy. I just really missed seeing you."

I gulped the biggest gulp of my life then had to force my eyes down towards the floor for a bit because there was just too much honesty in both his eyes and his tone and it was affecting the temperature and southern moisture levels more than I would have liked to admit.

Breathe again Toni Braxton!

"So you are still waiting then?" I asked after a deep exhale and a long pause because I needed time to recover from that sweet blow to my heart and vagina.

"I think we both know I never really stopped."

Thankfully that was the point in the conversation when I got called to another table so I left without a word, but by the time I was done handing out refills I knew what I wanted to say to him.

"You can only come once a week from now on," I said trying to lay out a set of ground rules to make the wait go more smoothly this time, but he just smiled.

"No dice. Best I can do is five days out of six," he offered like we were haggling at a garage sale.

"Kellen, you barely even finish your food so anything more than two days makes you look crazy."

"But I am about you so if the shoe fits, I'll wear it," he playfully reasoned, but I wasn't budging. "Alright four is my final offer."

"Three. One breakfast, lunch and a dinner. Take it or leave it," I offered with an outstretched hand to shake to let him know I was serious.

He looked down at it for a second before taking it into his. It was the first time we had ever done that so I wasn't surprised when he didn't let it go right away.

"Deal, but today doesn't count. The clock starts tomorrow," he said already looking for a way to cheat the system and that was when I knew for sure that I was already halfway in love with that man.

BYOB

AUGUST 12TH

6

Usually I could stand the sound of a little rain against my windowpane, but global warming really had shaken things up in recent years and the constant downpour had been driving me insane lately. Chicago had snow on the ground until mid-April so the rain showers reserved for spring decided to come down all summer long and ruin the plans that I'd *totally* planned on keeping.

Going out more was actually the first thing on my list, but I had continued paying it dust since it seemed to always be wet outside and I really did have my hands full with the two online business classes I'd enrolled in. I'd finished both with low As the week before, but I was still waiting for the perfect clear day to celebrate.

The forecast claimed that day would finally come the night before, but the crying clouds threw a tantrum and dramatically disagreed. In fact they had continued pouring down so badly that morning that I'd accidentally let them lull me back to sleep after silencing my alarm a couple times.

And what felt like a five-minute snooze nap was actually about fifty minutes so by the time I opened my eyes again, I was already late for work.

On the rare occasion that it happened I still took my time getting ready, but since Friday was Kellen's chosen day for his breakfast visits I rushed to get dressed in record time.

Despite the city's temperature rising for the summer months, things between him and I had pretty much remained stagnant. After shaking on how often he could visit the diner months ago, he kept his word and gave me the space that I'd asked for and even some investment advice to help speed things along.

Of course I was too scared to take it though so my money was sadly still in the same dusty account collecting pennies in interest every month. And for the first time in a while I was reminded of exactly why I needed to add *take more risks* to my list.

Hearing Jimmy's old trout mouth about respecting his time that morning was definitely not on my to-do list so I did my best to quietly stroll past his office without being seen. Unfortunately his door had been left wide open though so I was caught red handed as I stuffed the last of a muffin in my mouth and finished buttoning the top to my uniform.

I was never one to eavesdrop on private conversations so when I saw he was on the phone I went to shut it, but he didn't even bother with mincing his words when he had seen me standing there. He just continued with his talk about which day would work best for a potential buyer's inspection.

Now the bigger than average *For Sale* sign had been in the front window long before I'd set my sights on buying the joint. And every six months or so he would find an interested buyer, but they always pulled out for one reason or another. So the conversation alone didn't quite raise my antennas, but Jimmy smiling and doing a little dance when he ended it got the job done.

I almost couldn't believe my eyes. The man was literally never happy. Even when he went on his annual vacation to Florida with Paula at the end of every August all he did was complain about all the money he was missing from the diner being closed. Because instead of just letting us stay open he preferred to lose two weeks profit every year than let anybody else handle his money.

"Are you really doing it this time?"

"Don't see why not. They're coming Sunday and you best tell every broad in there to act like they got some sense if they want to keep working for these white folks when I'm gone," he warned me with a stern glare before getting excited again at the thought of finally being able to retire to Florida how he'd wanted to for years.

Before he broke his old mean face from smiling so hard, I handed him my phone with my bank app open and demanded that he look at the amount.

"Please don't do it. This is what I have in savings that I can give to you directly in cash. I know it's not nearly enough, but I'll get a loan to get you the rest by the time you come back from vacation. I swear."

"Get this lil' cheap, bright thang out my face, Lil' Bit," he teased me about my older phone before continuing, "I got a white man offering me almost double that."

"Yeah because of doctored pictures from back in the day. I don't know why you keep diner-fishing and wondering why it never works out," I teased him right back, but he clearly didn't like the joke being on him.

"You let me handle my business and you handle yours. And don't you owe me some money anyway?" he asked trying to sound convincing since he had seen how much I'd managed to squirl away over the past two and a half years.

"Come on Jimmy! Work with me! I'm family and you know nobody will love this place like I will," I whined as I threw my hands up in frustration.

"Nobody wants it more than I do. And no matter what they're offering you know like I know that nobody you bring in here will ever be dumb enough to take it on with this much debt so you better take this deal and run with it, you old geezer," I said playfully as I stuck out my hand hoping he would accept my official verbal offer.

He thought it over for a minute then reluctantly agreed to consider my offer valid but only on the condition that I was approved for a loan from the bank. That was all I needed to hear to immediately jump for joy because I'd already basically gotten a *pre*-preapproval when I laid out my costs and details for an assignment. All I had left to do was come up with an official business plan and set up a meeting.

I'm almost there!

"Pipe down and get to work. You're late," he reminded me before pointing to the door.

"Who cares? I'm the owner," I told him matter-of-factly while twirling and doing my own dance as I exited the small office.

"Not yet!" he yelled after me, but his words were a waste of breath since all I heard were bells chiming from my dreams coming true.

I headed straight to the kitchen to tell Lena the good news, but I couldn't get a word out when I found her in there complaining about how long her orders were taking.

"What's wrong with you?" I asked sounding concerned because she was never one to bitch to the line cooks. The food got there when it got there.

"Girl, I'm so over this day and it just started. I broke two nails and it feels like my period is coming early," she complained so I obnoxiously hugged her hoping to rub off some of my joy on her.

"Save that for yourself. You're about to be over the day too when you get out on the floor," she warned me. "You really blew it, bitch. We could've been living it up in the Hamptons with Diddy."

"What on earth are you talking about?" I asked a little grouchier than I intended to as I released her.

It wasn't even that I wasn't in the mood to play around anymore. I just wanted to talk about how I was finally about to get everything that was meant for me and she wasn't letting me.

"Jenna is out there serving Kellen right now. And I mean *serving* him, Wendy. Titties all in his face about to suffocate the man."

"You're lying," I accused her because no matter how long it took some days he always waited on me to take his order. I was over an hour late, but I still completely bypassed clocking in and said forget my apron as I ran over to peek through the server's window at him.

It took everything in me not to gasp at the scene before me. He was seated in my section *with coffee and food* smiling wide as all outside at whatever the hell she was saying.

Y'all wanna see a dead body?

And it would be justified too because it had been months since she started working here and she knew the rules now. Kellen was *my* regular and practically my sugar daddy so he was off limits.

Lena had been warning me for a while that some of the other girls were saying I needed to piss or get off the pot since I obviously didn't know what to do with him, but I wasn't expecting anybody to actually go for it. I knew I had to squash that shit immediately before he realized that unlike with me he could've actually been getting some sugar out of her.

"There's my favorite girl," he said when I came out of the kitchen with as neutral a face as I could muster up. "I waited as long as I could before uh…Jenna made me order something."

"Well I had to. Kel is getting as skinny as a post because you keep bringing him these dry wheat toast. At least put some butter and jam on them, girl," she teased me and I pretended to laugh along with them.

"Actually his name is *Kellen* not Kel and I can only bring him what he orders," I said through near-clenched teeth before her laugh turned awkward.

I saw the exact moment the lightbulb went off in Kellen's head that I was jealous of the attention she was giving him and I could tell he liked seeing that from me. He suddenly relaxed in his seat some and decided to watch the scene unfold with a little smug smile.

"Not if I have anything to say about it. Wendy's gonna have to learn to share you and we'll fatten you right up, *Kellen,*" she said putting emphasis on his name before clearing the table and sauntering off.

I felt foolish just standing there since his entire meal had already been taken care of and she was ringing up the check. I had no real reason to talk to him so I excused myself to finally go clock in but turned to run right into Lena who quietly threatened me through a smile for me to do it now or else.

I could tell from the look in her eyes that she was no longer playing with me and was finally ready to drag me from the window to the wall with how her day had been going. Plus I'd already made her lose all her little coins from the relationship racket she was running in the kitchen months ago so she was finally sick of me, my fears and excuses and the damn list.

That was it! The list. It wasn't until that very moment when I realized that it was completed and that I'd gotten my shit together…well kind of. I had been taking therapy much more seriously, I'd successfully completed my courses, I had made an informal but nonetheless a bid for the diner and dating Kellen would help me check off going out more so I was done. It truly was now or never.

I quickly turned to see Kellen's eyes raise from their fixed position on the back of my legs. He smiled guiltily at being caught as I took a seat into the booth opposite him.

"Hey you. Got any big plans this weekend?" I asked confidently even though I'd already felt my pits start to get moist.

"Uh nothing much. Just hanging out at home."

"Cool. Cool. So there's a new Greek restaurant that just opened a few blocks from here and I want to try it, but I hate having dinner alone especially somewhere that nice. We should go tomorrow night."

"Yeah I've heard good things and I've been wanting to try them too, but hold up. Wait a minute," he said before sitting up straight then checking his reflection in the napkin holder. "I'm not just about to let you breeze by this historical moment with no fanfare. Are *you* Wendella Bell asking *me* Kellen Turner out on a date? Is that what's happening here?" he asked being silly and I tried real hard to keep a straight face since his smile was big enough for the both of us.

Mm hm. That's exactly what's happening.

"No. I was just letting you know that I would be there in case you wanted to maybe be there too. That's all." I nervously picked at a piece of lint from my collar until he spoke again.

"Well you know I would love to be there, but actually I just remembered that I do have something this weekend so we'll have to do it some other time."

I couldn't tell if he was joking or not until he gestured for me to say something so I knew he'd meant it.

"Oh okay. I probably won't even go either. I've never even had Greek food before...so yeah maybe some other time," I suggested as I slid out of the booth and tried to pick up my face and my feelings. Obviously he'd been waiting around for this day to come so that he could return the favor and punish me for making him wait so long.

Men could be such bit--

"Wait I know it's short notice, but I'm free tonight if you are," he said after grabbing my hand and pulling me over to his side.

Okay never mind. False alarm!

"She is," Lena said walking by with plates in both hands not even pretending that she wasn't listening in. "Pick her up here at seven and you better treat my cousin real nice, Kellen."

"Trust me I will. She's in good hands," he said to her but kept his eyes fixed upwards on mine. "So we're really doing this?" he asked like he wanted to make sure he wasn't just imagining it.

"Yeah looks like it."

"Alright well it's kind of last minute to make reservations at the Greek spot so is there somewhere else you want to go?" he asked before almost knocking over the napkin holder. Him being nervous oddly calmed me and made me smile.

He had clearly been caught off guard by all of this too because his usual smoothness was gone and replaced with a bumbling guy.

"No. We can just do something casual like dinner and a movie this time. I've been wanting to see you out of those suits for too long now anyway." I didn't realize how weird the words sounded until they were already out of my mouth. "I-I mean in *other* more casual clothes. Not like naked or anything." Now he was smiling again.

"I know what you mean. I've been wanting to see you out of your uniform too."

"And in other clothes?" I tried finishing his sentence for him, but he'd clearly meant it exactly how it had sounded.

"Yeah if you say so," he said flirtatiously before swiping my pen for a second to write his cell number on the back of his business card.

It hadn't even dawned on me just how long we had been tiptoeing around each other's feelings when we literally hadn't even exchanged phone numbers yet. He must have realized the same since he celebrated finally being locked in even if it did say *Kellen Never Kel*.

Before leaving he made sure to leave a decent tip for Jenna but still snuck my usual into my pocket on his way out and instead of telling me that he would see me tomorrow he ended with, "I'll see you tonight, beautiful."

I know his dick is big. I know it. I know it's big.

I floated through the rest of my shift. I didn't know how me or Lena managed to get any tips at all because we both neglected the hell out of our tables trying to mentally put together a good date night look.

Suddenly every piece of clothing I owned was ugly or didn't fit quite right until we got to a thrifted green sundress with small sunflower buttons on it. The tattered tags were still attached when I bought it years ago so I knew it'd never been worn before, but it looked like it was made for me as it draped my body and gave the illusion that I was curvier than I actually was.

Prancing around my apartment I looked like a rich southern belle on a hot summer day, wholesome in theory but unpredictable once the honey whiskey came out. I knew the entire look was hitting all the right notes when Lena stopped in her tracks after coming out of the bathroom.

"I love it! It's giving Shea Butter Baby and 'You can spin my wheel of fortune if the price is right!'"

"No no no. There will be no spinning anything tonight. Just getting to know each other and that's it," I said trying to convince us both.

"He's rich and fine. What else do you need to know?" she asked as she started gathering her things to leave before I could ask for help putting all my dresses and shoes back where they belonged.

I alternated between feeling nervous and excited but surprisingly more normal than anything. Things were really turning around for me and the only change I could pinpoint was simply thinking more positively the past few months. I was really about to own the diner and maybe even have the kind of man that I had always dreamed about having.

I didn't want to get too far ahead of myself with either though because whenever I started enjoying my dreams too much it always seemed like reality would come out of nowhere to wake me up.

At precisely seven on the dot my phone thudded about on my vanity. I knew it was Kellen calling to let me know that he had arrived so I fluffed up my half up and half down hair once more then let the doorknob hit me.

In anticipation of the rain I'd brought an umbrella with me, but the clouds were calm and clear for miles and the sun had popped out for an appearance. The summer evening air was warm and welcoming as I stepped out into it.

I knew I confused him by leaving out of my separate side door instead of emerging from inside the diner like he expected, but the confusion he wore seamlessly transitioned to appreciation as I got closer.

"Wow," he said through a smile that would seemingly never end at seeing me in something other than my pink work getup.

"I know! This is so weird. I can see your little legs," I squealed as I took him and his casual clothes in. He wore all white, a sleeveless button-down shirt and shorts that were just short enough to be interesting but not too short.

"Little? Little where? Wendy, I'm too thick," he said playfully as he looked down at himself and brushed off imaginary dirt.

"Oh good so we're both delusional then because I swear I'm getting thick all the time too meanwhile it's still business as usual over here."

"That's different. I think you've already got the perfect amount of business," he shamelessly complimented my body with a quick nibble of his bottom lip.

"Are you admitting that you've been minding my business then, Kellen?"

"I mean it's kind of hard not to since..." he began, but I finished his statement.

"I know. Since my business is all out on front street in there," I said as I smoothed out a wrinkle in the much longer midi dress.

"Alright that's enough about business. You ready to finally go play?" he asked as he stepped aside to open the door to an old school cherry red Corvette.

I waited for an explanation because I had definitely seen his car countless times before and it was bigger and black and I don't know...not that.

"I've had it for a few weeks now, but this is the first time I'm actually taking it out for a drive."

"Oh. Aren't you too young to be having a mid-life crisis already?" I asked since I now knew he was just about five years older than me.

He just smiled then explained that he thought they were arguably more sensible than newer cars because the lack of power steering and automatic brakes forced drivers to be more alert on the road. All I'd heard were no brakes though so he still wasn't getting me into that thing.

"They're manual and it's safe. Trust me. Now that I got a date with you, I'm not trying to leave here any sooner than I have to. I've just always wanted one but thought it wasn't really practical until now."

"What made it practical now?" I asked curiously as I finally let him help me into the passenger side.

"Nothing in particular, but you only live once, you know?"

He drove with the top down, but he was considerate and went slower so that my hair wouldn't blow in the wind too much. I had never ridden through the city in a two-seater before, but I found it to be quite the experience. I almost felt like I was suddenly living inside B-roll footage from *Grease*.

A sudden rumble in my tummy reminded me that I had been too anxious to eat all day so I asked if we were doing dinner or the movie first. Thankfully he said that he had packed a picnic because we were going to Boat Cinema at DuSable Harbor. I'd never been there before, but I knew from where we parked that the part we were headed to wasn't open to the public.

"Are we lost?"

"No. We're going to watch from my boat. It's a little trick I learned from my dad. You can see and hear everything right from the dock," he said like he had done it a million times before.

"Wait stealing from a damn yacht, Kellen? That's a new low. Why are rich people so cheap?" I cracked on him.

"First of all it's not a yacht. It's a midrange cruiser. Nothing major," he said trying to appear humble. "And who ever said I was 'rich' anyway?" he asked like it was such an absurd thought.

"Well poor people definitely don't tip like you do and you just have that 'I know exactly where each fork goes look' to you."

"But you know where each fork goes too."

"Yeah from waitressing at a high end restaurant one summer. It is not the same."

The short films that played before the feature film started up so we quickly boarded and got settled. The millennial in me resisted the urge to yell out *I'm on a boat, bitch!* right when he began unpacking a big picnic basket.

"I know you said you like to cook before, but that's not exactly my calling so this was the best I could do on such short notice," he said preparing me to expect the worst when it was anything but.

There were fancy cheeses, fruits and meats, basically a nice spread with several options in case I didn't like something and even chocolate tarts for dessert. He'd remembered that they were my favorites because it was the only thing he'd ever seen me eat inside the diner when we had them for dessert specials.

"You did all of this yourself?"

"Yeah of course I did," he said sounding like it was a complete lie before admitting the truth. "Well I did ask a nice old lady in Whole Foods to help me. She said she hoped we had a good time, but just in case we didn't she has two single granddaughters my age."

"Oh so you're a hot commodity in the diner and in grocery aisles? I sure hope I can impress you tonight."

"Pretty sure you did that months ago," he said casually while handing me a small plate which I immediately planned to use for a couple tarts.

"Wait. Save them for the end. Trust me it'll be even better with the wine after you've had the savory saltiness from the food," he said simply enough, but I found myself getting turned on by how he described the flavors as I whined because they looked so good.

"Am I gonna have to teach you a thing or two about being patient?" he teased me before struggling to pop the cork on an old heavy looking bottle of wine.

"Oh so now you're an expert on waiting?"

"Definitely. You know how hard it was to see you so much and know that I couldn't have you?" he asked through a sexy grunt as he concentrated extra hard to get the bottle open.

I was glad it took him a while too since I probably would have toppled the boat from jumping his bones if he dared make eye contact with me after saying that.

It was much cooler out on the water and we were both sleeveless so luckily he had thought ahead to bring a blanket though it wasn't very big. I knew he was a born strategist so I was sure it was so we could share it and almost cuddle. As always though he made sure to be a true gentleman as we got comfortable and he kept his hands where I could see them.

The full-length movie finally began and I was pleased to see that it was the original *Carmen Jones* with Dorothy Dandridge and Harry Belafonte. I'd always wanted to see it but never quite got around to it for some reason.

Literally from scene one I loved everything about it. The music was amazing. It had its funny moments and the aesthetic was like nothing I'd ever seen before. It must have been a restored version too because the color was so vibrant that it made me want to somehow go buy Carmen's exact shade of red lipstick.

The rain clouds had been teasing their return all throughout the movie's runtime, but they waited right until we were almost to the end to start showing out again. Across the harbor you could see all the people in the smaller boats coming in before the drizzle got too heavy so Kellen and I followed their lead.

We packed everything up as quickly as we could then made a run for it to his car. He knew that I still had work in the morning so one look at his watch said it was time to get me home anyway so we ended the night enjoying the tarts on the drive over. And he had been right. Even without another glass of wine to go with them they were even better after the wait.

"This was fun. Why oh why did it take us so long to finally do this?" I asked him sarcastically when he walked me to my door like I wasn't the one holding things up for months.

My big umbrella did a great job shielding us from the light rain, but it did nothing for all the warm feelings that were also falling on us from the sky as we made googly eyes under the moon.

"Well I mean you all but told me you were creeped out by me so…" he said then let his words drift off with the wind.

"I never said creeped out."

"I believe the word *uncomfortable* was used…" he said playfully before looking down to meet my eyes. "Are you comfortable now?" I nodded. "Good. That's all I wanted."

"Mm. Is that really all you wanted?" I challenged because I could for sure name at least one other thing that he was certainly after.

"I think what or rather *who* I want has been well documented by now. What do you want, Wendy?" he asked so smoothly that I practically felt my panties removing themselves for him. I had to clear my throat to bring me back into the fold.

"Um…I already told you. For all of this to be mine," I gestured over towards the diner to get the heat off of me since we were at the end of the night, but it was still young enough for endless possibilities.

"What's the biggest hurdle keeping you from making it yours?" he asked as if it wasn't already obvious.

"Well first I have to officially get approved for a loan, but I talked to somebody today and I actually go in for a meeting next week. Now my credit is a little shaky, but I've been saving every penny for years so hopefully that'll help with the down payment part."

"And what's your backup plan if that doesn't work out for you?"

It was a simple and straightforward question, but I paused for a while because I honestly hadn't even thought of it not working out how I wanted it to. I felt naïve all of a sudden and for the first time all night I was reminded that I was on a date with somebody who already had an extremely successful business.

"All of my eggs are in this one basket so I guess I don't really have a backup plan. I bet you think that's kind of foolish, huh?"

"No. Not at all. I've seen you work long enough to know that you love this place even when you hate it. And I have a feeling that everything's gonna work out and one day soon I'll be ordering a cup of coffee in your diner," he assured me before asking what I'd be calling it after removing Jimmy's name.

"I'm thinking of going back to Mae's, but too bad Wendy's is already taken, right?" I joked and we shared a laugh. "Maybe I'll take a page from both of our parents and call it Wellen's since you're practically an investor at this point," I teased him about his tips.

"I don't know about all of that, but I do like the sound of putting you and me together," he said forwardly.

I checked the time to see that it was just about half past ten so I knew that it was time for me to be heading inside. I stood then attempted to give him a quick hug goodnight, but I didn't object to him letting his hands hang out on my waist for a while.

"Thanks for being good company tonight."

"Are we calling it a night already?" he asked hinting about wanting to finally come up to my apartment.

"Uh yeah it's kind of a disaster up there right now. It takes a long time and a lot of mess to look this basic," I self-depreciated even though I actually thought I looked really cute.

"You and I both know that you've never looked basic a day in your life," he complimented before slowly leaning in for a kiss. Our lips briefly brushed against each other's and I almost let it happen, but at the last second I chickened out and connected with his cheek instead.

"I like to take things slowly, okay? Maybe next time if you're lucky," I told him letting it be known that I did enjoy myself enough to want to get together again.

"That's alright with me. I think you know by now that I'll wait however long it takes for you," he said with sincerity, but the look in his eyes and a quick lick of his lips sent a shiver up my back that made me feel like I was in the middle of winter.

I warmed back up though when he leaned back in to kiss my cheek then let his lips boldly but still gently fall down to my neck and collarbone.

"Mm mn. Goodnight Kellen never Kel," I laughed out as I put space between us because I knew what he was trying to do and I had already been tempted enough for one night.

"Alright goodnight for real," he said before placing one more sweet kiss on the top of my head and telling me how the night had been everything he could've hoped for.

"It was definitely worth the wait," he said with a look in his eyes I hadn't seen before. It wasn't necessarily happy or even sexual. It just looked like he really fucking meant that. I didn't even think he was trying to get up my dress anymore, but boy did I suddenly want him there so I pulled back for good.

"Yeah maybe we can finish the movie next time. I know I'm about a hundred years late, but I really want to see them finally get together." For some reason he reacted strangely to that so I had to ask why.

"That's not exactly how *Carmen Jones* ends."

"Really? I thought it was supposed to be like a love conquers all, happily ever after type of story. What happened?" I asked curiously, but he hesitated before I assured him that I didn't mind spoilers.

"Well I don't want to give it all away, but they couldn't have a happily ever after because one of them dies at the end."

DINE AND DASH
AUGUST 19ᵀᴴ
7

You couldn't tell me that after a first date like the one I'd had with Kellen Turner that we wouldn't instantly become attached at the hip. It'd been one for the books so naturally I abandoned all common sense and began thinking too far ahead about becoming relationship goals and sharing the story of how we'd met in the diner.

However, the unexpected had happened and the fairytale ending I'd envisioned turned out to be just another cautionary tale instead. I literally hadn't heard a peep out of him since he'd pulled off after our date a week ago. Not even a text to say that he'd made it home safely.

For the first few days I was still deep in denial about it. Like maybe it was some new dating thing to cool off for a while to not seem too desperate. I was a little rusty in this department after all so I tried to give him some grace. But by closing time Wednesday, his usual night to stop by for dinner, I had gotten the message loud and clear—he was never coming back.

To say that I was confused would be an understatement. Because yeah we didn't have sex or even really kiss, but the chemistry was still off the charts. But even more than I was confused, I was hurt. And I knew I was letting myself feel way too much for somebody I'd only been out with once, but it was because everything he'd done leading up to our date had me convinced that he was different.

For five months Kellen had me living in another dimension. I'd gotten so high off of the thought of us and how he was "investing" in me and my future when really those tips were nothing but pocket change to him and he'd just intended on them being a down payment for access to me sexually. That shit hurt on a different level.

But as messed up as it was, I pretty much just had to accept it because there was nothing else I could do about it anyway. Lena was still unconvinced that he was ghosting me for no reason though and even almost got me worried that maybe something had happened to him.

I had to admit it was a possibility though especially when I thought about the lack of brakes on his new car and how we'd shared a couple bottles of wine that night. Also if he were to be hurt and laid up in a hospital somewhere it wasn't exactly like I was an emergency contact that would be notified.

But before I embarrassed myself any further by frantically calling every hospital in Gotham searching for Bruce Wayne, I decided to reach out to him directly, albeit anonymously, first to see if he answered. I'd felt like I was back in high school with the phone pressed to my ear that morning, but at the very least acting young and dumb had gotten me some answers.

He'd picked up on the fourth ring sounding good and sleepy but also very much alive and well so it just was what it was at that point. Obviously I had been mistaken and he just wasn't that into me.

Before knowing him work had always been the perfect distraction from whatever was bothering me in my personal life, but he had entwined himself so well with that part of my day that even it didn't stop me from thinking about him. Every day for my entire shift I looked up every time somebody new came in somehow both hoping that it would and wouldn't be him.

Even during my meeting with the loan officer at my bank, I kept imagining if his office was even nicer than hers was when I should have been paying attention to all the signs that she would be rejecting my application.

She was *really* nice about it though. She stressed that the presentation and paperwork were completed well beyond bank standards, but that my payment history was poor and that I just didn't have enough personal collateral to borrow such a large amount.

And of course she remembered to smile when she encouraged me to apply again in a year or two when I had somehow magically fixed those things. I politely returned her smile, thanked her for her time and headed for the door feeling defeated but trying like hell not to show it.

All I could think about was Lena telling me to lie, lie and then lie some more when I was filling out the forms. I couldn't wait to tell her that as usual she had been right.

Why oh why did I ever think it was a good idea to tell a hwite person the truth?

Hopelessness wasn't exactly the right fit for the feeling I had on my way out. It was much lower than that. The further I got out the door the further my dream of owning the diner slipped through my fingertips so by that point I knew if I didn't fight for it right then and there then it would probably never happen.

Forget a year or two, in that moment I decided to turn right back around and let her know that there was a person with a story behind all those details that made me an undesirable loan candidate.

I had done a gorgeous minimalist makeup look and wrestled with my hair to get a sleek bun for the meeting. My business casual clothes were neat and pressed, but it all proved to be for nothing because the things that I'd planned on saying to her when I barged back in were anything but professional.

"My payment history is poor because for years I didn't know a thing about credit except that when my mother died I was forced to survive off of it. I don't have more collateral because I'm a waitress and unfortunately lots of people think tipping is optional even after I break my damn back to give them the absolute best service money can buy!"

"Ms. Bell I'm so sorry about all of your…hardships. I truly am but--" she began before I cut her off because I was nowhere near finished.

"You want to know how you can be sure I'll pay this loan back on time? Because this is the only thing I've ever been passionate about in my life. Because this diner is all I have left. And if you don't take a chance on me today then my uncle is going to sell it to a stranger soon and I'll never be able to get it back!"

Aside from my chest heaving up and down from breathing so hard, there was almost no movement between the two of us until she removed her glasses and spoke more sympathetically than before.

If my life was a movie that speech would've been enough to secure the loan, but I could tell that my real world answer would still be no.

"Ms. Bell, I'll admit that your passion is very admirable, but unfortunately passion is not one of the criteria that we base lending decisions on. Now I do have some resources for women and minorities that I can give you that might fast-track the approval timeline, but as for today you're still considered a significant risk and there's nothing else I can do for you."

I had been unprofessional enough by storming into her office so even though I didn't plan on using her resources I sat tight while she gathered them for me. On my way out for real this time I spotted a checklist stapled to the front of a manilla folder.

The universe had jokes, I thought as I laughed bitterly to myself then tossed it in the trash before I could get out of the building. Lists hadn't helped me get anywhere faster lately but to some hurt feelings so I wasn't jumping through anymore hoops to complete another one.

The day had begun cool, dark and rainy so I wanted nothing more than to crawl back into bed when I got back to the diner at lunch time, but instead I went straight to Jimmy's office to ask him for more time on our arrangement. I knew the potential buyer had come in and done a quick appraisal the other day, but he still hadn't gotten back to Jimmy yet which gave me one last opportunity to seek out a loan from a different source.

Because even though the woman didn't tell me what I wanted to hear, it was still just one opinion and I'd learned recently not to put all my eggs into one basket in every facet of life. Surely there was another bank or lender in the city that would gladly empty my savings for the deal.

Continuing my stupid theme of being honest for the day, I laid everything out on the table but assured Jimmy that since I had nothing to do for the next two weeks while he was on vacation that I would search day and night for a solution.

He didn't seem to think it was a good idea though and strangely told me that I should actually get out and enjoy myself for a change during the break.

"Maybe this is all for the best."

"What? How can you say that? You know how bad I want this."

"Well life done taught me that we can't always get what we want. And I just got word even after the walkthrough the buyer still wants to gone 'head with the deal so that's that," he said definitively like he had already made up his mind long before I'd come in.

"Jimmy no! You can't. I'll match his offer. Whatever it is. I just need you to hold out a little while longer, Jimmy please!" I begged him feeling the tears gather in the corners of my eyes.

"I'm sorry Lil' Bit, but what's done is done. You're my favorite sister's baby girl and I love you, do anything for you, but this here is business. Try not to take it personal, you hear me?"

I'd definitely heard him loud and clear even though I didn't want to so I nodded and wiped my face like he expected before any tears could fall because I knew they made him uncomfortable. He was right. It was business and no matter how much I wanted to be mad at him, I couldn't be. After all this was the same man who had taken me in and given me a place to stay and--

"Wait, if you've sold the diner then that includes the upstairs apartment. Jimmy, where the hell am I supposed to live now?!" I asked finally raising my voice because I hadn't even considered that part of the sale until then.

"Now *this* is where it gets personal, Lil' Bit. I know you been saving for a rainy day so don't go complaining now that it's storming," he said coldly as he got up to shut the window from the fresh rain pouring in. "You'll be alright. You tough like your mama was."

Yeah but I shouldn't have to be. Nobody should.

Even though I had no more words for him I sat there for a full minute literally just in shock. Well the part about the words was a lie because before I left I did apparently need to ask how soon I needed to be moved out. He basically just told me that by the time he came back from Florida he would need me packed up and gone.

For the third time that day, I accepted defeat but left grateful that there were no bridges on the way up to get changed for my shift. Because for the first time in years I was tempted to stand on top of one, lean forward a little then let gravity do its thing.

It was all good just a week ago...

I'd foolishly went from thinking that I could have it all to losing everything in the blink of an eye. No loan. No diner. No apartment. No Kellen.

I felt like my world was ending and it wasn't even noon yet. I told myself that calling in sick would be stupid since Jimmy knew for a fact I was just fine, but I should have done anything but clock in that day because I was not a good enough actress to put on the brave face needed to tough it out until quitting time.

Literally ten minutes on the clock and a glass of spilled milk almost sent me spiraling. Before I knew it I had snapped on a random man for goofing around and making me knock it over on a woman in Lena's section. I didn't even bother staying to help clean it up because I knew if I was on the floor for one more second that I would scream.

Crying in the bathroom wasn't something that was unusual around here because the theme screamed *I Love Lucy* and practically demanded melodrama. But crying in the walk-in freezer? That was Emmy-winning dramatics and usually only done by me.

It'd been a while since I had a full-blown panic attack at work. Usually I could feel them coming so I would take deep breaths then hang out in there for a few minutes until my skin was no longer hot to the touch.

But today it was like I needed to feel every bit of it since this was the only way I could release my suppressed emotions. The cooks had clearly seen me come in so when the door swung open a little while later I knew it could only be one person coming to check on me.

"Lena, can you hold me for a minute?" I asked her sounding just as pathetic as I probably looked, but I didn't care. I just really needed somebody to rock me like my mama used to.

It had been over a decade since I'd last felt her loving arms wrapped around me, but I still missed them just the same. Luckily for me Lena honored my request then squatted down next to me on the cold floor. She had been well aware of my disorder, but she'd never seen me up close and personal when I was like that so I could tell I had scared her a little.

I did my best to breathe through it all and ground myself until I felt comfortable enough to actually talk to her about what was going on.

"I take it the meeting for the loan didn't go too good?" she guessed since she had let me borrow her car to get there.

"That's not even the half of it. Jimmy already sold the diner behind my back and I have to be moved out by the end of the break."

"Are you fucking serious?" she asked so angrily after a genuine gasp that I didn't even have the heart to throw in Kellen answering his phone earlier and being okay after all.

"As a heart attack."

"Well don't worry about that. You know if you need somewhere to stay--" she began, but I immediately cut her off.

"Thank you, but I'll figure something out. I will not be on the couch listening to you and Greg bouncing off the walls all night." She just laughed because she knew it was true.

"I'm glad you know nothing stops us from getting it in," she joked then got serious again. "But just know that it's there if you need it."

"I know and thank you for being the best family and friend I've ever had." I hugged her tightly before asking a question that I couldn't even answer myself.

"How did my life end up like this? I was finally feeling like I was getting some footing by being here, but now the rug is just getting ripped from underneath me again. I swear I was this close to having everything."

"And you still very much are. All of this is just a stepping stone, Wendy. You've always been a fighter and you never give up. This is not the end for you," she said as she rubbed my back in support. "As a matter of fact, let's go to Pet World later and get a bunch of mice. I bet they'll sell this bitch right back to Jimmy when they see *Ratatouille* and his crew running around here."

At first I gave her a small grin for her effort to get me to laugh, but since I was already at my lowest I decided to be honest with her about the thing with Kellen.

"I can't believe I actually thought he was one of the good ones. And what's worse is he took the tips with him right when I need them the most. I gotta move and pay actual rent prices now!" I joked and got another chuckle out of her. "It's my fault though because I knew better. Men like him don't date waitresses. They'll sleep with us. But date? Not gonna happen."

"Didn't Matt Damon wife a waitress?" she asked predictably bringing up the exception to the rule.

"Yeah well *Black* Damon certainly out acted Matt here, but he still didn't want the role as my man," I spat bitterly.

"Well who said y'all had to date anyway? You had all the dates and foreplay in here for months. You were s'posed to just buss it open on the boat because you know we all wanted to know if *Richie Rich* tipped good between the sheets too," she said mannishly causing me to roll my eyes.

"No not sleeping with him was the smartest thing I could've done. And this is why I only concern myself with money because money doesn't lie and it can never disappoint me. I'm officially off of men forever so go ahead and bring a few stray cats to my housewarming party," I joked attempting to laugh through the pain, but I still couldn't muster up a real one.

"Wendy, no you better not use this as an excuse to keep you from opening up again. You never have any fun! Everything is always about you saving up to buy this old raggedy place. Do something for you, bitch then figure out your next moves. You've got two weeks off work, but all you're gonna do is mope around up there and scroll on IG until your thumb cramps up," she said reading me up and down and all I could do was listen as I wiped my face because she hadn't told a lie yet.

I let her words digest some before telling her that I was finally ready to head back out on the floor, but it wasn't until we stood up that I realized what she had been wearing the whole time. To keep warm she'd borrowed one of the ugly Christmas sweaters from our lost and found box and it looked ridiculously cute on her.

Now I hadn't genuinely smiled in days, but seeing her usually stylish self with Rudolph on her body in the middle of August brought out a laugh from the depths of my soul and it took forever to finally subside.

"I'm glad this is so funny to you 'cause if I catch a cold in here or cooties from this sweater then I'm taking you to *Judge Mathis*," she threatened as we emerged from the kitchen feeling refreshed and ready to work.

I was behind her so she blocked my view of what had stopped her in her tracks, but whatever it was upset her on sight.

"I know this negro did not just..." Lena began under her breath before I saw *him* with my very own eyes.

And obviously I didn't intend to stare a hole into him, but I almost couldn't look away since I had never seen him looking so regular before. He had on sweats and a dad hat and looked like he was coming from a baseball game or whatever the hell bosses did on their days off.

I was immediately tempted to go back in the freezer and put myself on ice again, but I decided I was no longer literally or figuratively crying over spilled milk today. Especially not for some slimy frog that had been hopping around and masquerading as Prince Charming.

Kellen never Kel had clearly shown up with a specific mission in mind because me ignoring and working around him wasn't the deterrent that I thought it'd be. He was even arrogant enough to help himself to an empty table in my section when Lena tried to spare his life by begrudgingly offering him a counter seat.

After a while Jenna's thirsty self noticed what was going on and tried to take his order, but just like any other day he said that he was waiting on me. I just laughed to myself because I knew hell would freeze over before I ever served Kellen Turner again.

The temperature down there had to have dropped a few degrees by the time Jimmy came out to use the restroom at the peak of the lunch rush. He noticed a few folks waiting to be seated and a still unserved Kellen taking up an entire table.

Jimmy let me know that niece or not if I played with his final full day of profits that I would be out of a job before the new owner could take over. Without a place to stay soon I knew I needed this last day of tips more than ever so I approached his table but kept my eyes on my booklet.

"Hi. Can I take your order?" I asked with as little emotion in my voice as possible. I wouldn't even give him the fake happy greeting that I usually put on when Jimmy was near.

"Can we talk?"

"Only if it's about your order, *Kel*," I said just to upset him, but he didn't even bother reacting.

"I already ate before I came," he said simply enough, but it made me want to look up to see his face. His hat was pulled down low over his eyes, but he still seemed relaxed and unbothered which was more than I could say for myself.

"Then what else could you possibly be here for?" I asked more coldly than I'd intended to, but it was fitting for the predicament that he'd put us in.

"Look I know that was you who called and hung up on me this morning," he accused and even though I was certain he couldn't have known for sure I didn't deny it. "Can you take a break so we can go talk?"

"No. As you can see we're really busy right now so if you're not going to order anything then you should probably just go," I said before gesturing to Jimmy that I was no longer the reason he didn't have any food or beverage.

"Alright fine. Bring me a short stack and I guess I'll just keep waiting until you're ready then. It's not like I'm new to it," he said after sighing like I was the one annoying him at his job. It took everything in me not to smash one of the freshly baked cherry pies I'd just set out in his lying ass face.

"Oh you mean like how you said you would wait the other night? Because how fucked up is it that you pretend to be this great man in here for months only to stop speaking to me when I wouldn't sleep with you on the first fucking date, Kellen?!" I asked loud enough to get the attention of just about everybody in the place.

"Is that what you really think of me after all of this time?!" he asked raising his voice to the same volume as mine as he stood up from his seat.

"Yes because what the hell else am I supposed to think after you just up and disappeared?"

He was about to answer me before he suddenly realized that we had a diner full of staff and customers hanging on to the edge of their seats just waiting to see how the production we were putting on would end. Obviously wanting some privacy, he grabbed a hold of me then whisked me to the back staircase where we had hung out alone months before.

"Kellen. I really don't have time for this today so you need to make it quick before--"

"Wendy sit your ass down and listen to me right now!" he said in a tone that he had never used with me.

For obvious reasons I didn't respond well to men showing any signs of aggression, but I could tell that Kellen's frustration wasn't the violent kind. He just wanted to be heard so I decided to let him borrow my ears though I wasn't convinced that they would hear something to mend the hurt he'd been responsible for.

I took a seat on the stairs, but he leaned against the wall in front of me with his hands in his pockets, hopefully digging for the truth for a change.

"I'm sorry I didn't call, alright? There's no excuse for that. It's just…You and I don't have a future together and I shouldn't have led you on to believe that we could have one."

Well fuck you too then!

His tone wasn't harsh at all, but just like with the loan officer from the bank I realized that it didn't matter how kindly you said something that was fucked up. It was still fucked up!

I knew then that continuing to listen would just do more damage instead of giving me the closure I was after so I got up to leave.

"Wait wait," he said stopping me before I could cross back over to the diner. "Wendy, the reason we don't have a future together is not because I don't want to be with you. It's because I'm dying!" he blurted out before he lost my attention.

"Well that's a new one. Look if you didn't want to see me again you didn't have to come up with some elaborate ass lie. I already knew this wouldn't really turn into anything and--"

"Wendy!"

"What?!"

"Listen to me!" he yelled out with even more frustration than before. "I'm selfish and I fucked everything up, but I've never lied to you and I'm not about to start now. The other night you were making all of these plans for us to go on more dates and when I got home I panicked.

Because as much as I wanted there to be I knew it was too late for other dates.”

The emotion in his voice and the heaviness of his words finally began to sink in as I stepped backwards until my butt connected with the stairs again.

“Why are you…I mean w-what's wrong with you?” I asked looking around for any obvious signs of illness. He looked the same as he always did though, a little thinner than when we'd met but still healthy.

“It's my heart. I have HCM,” he said like I was supposed to know what that meant. “Hypertrophic cardiomyopathy. It just means it's hard for my heart to pump blood.”

“Well why don't you just get a transplant or something?”

“That's a good idea. You know I actually hadn't thought of that,” he said sarcastically before continuing. “I've been on the list for years, but I'm a 1B not 1A which is medical jargon for saying I'm fucked but not as fucked as the first priority people who have to stay in the hospital full-time. The writing is on the wall though. The meds aren't working like they used to so it's just a matter of *when* not *if* now.”

“But you have money. *Real* money. Couldn't you like…I don't know do something funny to get one?” I asked because I'd always figured rich people had access to all kinds of shady black-market stuff that the rest of us didn't. He found my apparent naivety endearing and reached out and touched my face.

"That's just Hollywood stuff. Anybody who gets taken off the transplant list without dying is asking for trouble and I'm not trying to get more time just to spend it in jail," he said which made a lot of sense.

"I thought about telling you all of this months ago, but I didn't want to put that big of a burden on somebody I barely knew."

"So then why are you telling me now?"

"Because you called. And that's when I knew I couldn't just pretend like these past five months with you didn't happen. I had written you a letter explaining everything, but you deserve to know the truth while I'm still here," he said before handing me his phone.

I was confused at the documents on the screen until I realized what they were.

"Kellen, this is a will saying you're leaving everything you have to me." I looked up to him to make sure that what I was seeing was accurate. "How do I even know this is real?" I asked before seeing that it had been filed with the Cook County Probate Court.

It was real, alright. He had left every red cent to Wendella "Wendy" Bell of Chicago, Illinois. Something else even more important than my name caught my eye after skimming over the entire thing though.

"This was filed in March. How long have you been planning this?"

"Since the night we met when you told me everything would be okay. Because I knew it wouldn't be. I just didn't have the heart to tell you that then. At first I kept coming back because I just wanted to get a better feel for you to make sure I wasn't completely out of my mind to be leaving everything to a stranger just because she was nice to me when she didn't have to be. But every morning after that night I found myself actually looking forward to my day again because I was looking forward to seeing you," he said as he grabbed my hand in his.

"I could've gotten a decent cup of coffee anywhere in the city, Wendy, but I came back to this diner every day for you and that feeling that only you had ever given me."

"But if you knew you were dying this whole time then why would you even start waiting for me?"

"Because waiting for you made me feel like I was actually alive again, not just biding my time. And I already told you I was crazy over you so I don't know why you're acting surprised," he said playfully even though his actions showed how much weight was actually behind the words.

"But what about your family? Your friends? Literally anybody besides the waitress you met five months ago?!" I exclaimed, stupidly trying to talk him out of something that I should have been on mute about.

"My parents are long gone and it's just me. I haven't told anybody else about what's going on because I don't want people feeling bad for me or acting different or even worse, coming around just to get in my will. I've already done what I wanted to do for the people who've been good to me and hopefully they'll remember me when I was at my best."

He looked like he was finally tired of standing as he walked over and took a seat next to me.

"Why so serious?" he asked being silly and quoting The Joker. "I thought every woman wanted a dying man to leave her some money."

"Yeah well it's different because you're not old and decrepit and I actually really like you," I told him honestly before taking a deep breath and just going for it. I put my hands on the back of his neck and urged him to bring his lips down to mine.

"You sure you're ready for this? I know how much you like making me wait for stuff," he said sarcastically before removing his hat so that there would be nothing keeping our lips from colliding for the first time.

On impact his already felt like home. They were full and juicy and played well with mine as I gently sucked on each one while he let go of any inhibitions he might have had and moaned right into my mouth.

"Damn. This is how I know it's really the end because I'm getting one last hurrah before I go," he said as I was still recovering from the sweet but very sensual smooch. "You want to get out of here?"

"I can't. I still have to get back to work," I said since becoming the beneficiary to more Ms than I had fingers and toes for still seemed surreal and far off.

"Actually you don't," he said vaguely before I asked what he meant by that. "I promise this is the last thing I'll spring on you today."

He leaned over closer to me again to get a folded-up piece of paper from his pocket. When I unfolded it I saw that it was a copy of a bill of sale for the diner and Kellen Turner was listed as the owner.

"Wait you're the one who bought the diner?!"

"Calm down. It's part of my estate now so it's yours just like everything else," he promised before I explained that I was still upset since more than anybody he knew how much I wanted to buy it for myself.

"Yeah well at the rate you were going, we would've both been dead by the time you could afford it. I only jumped on it because there was another serious offer on the table."

I opened my mouth to speak because I had more to say and complain about until I realized that I actually didn't. He had just done the most selfless thing ever for me so I wouldn't let my pride get in the way of letting him know how much I appreciated it deep down.

"I don't even know what to say about all of this. It's unreal and thank you just doesn't feel like enough," I began before wrapping my arms around him, "but thank you so much, Kellen. I promise I'll never call you Kel again!" I squealed out which made him chuckle into my neck.

The door separating us from the diner suddenly swung open and out came Lena who looked surprised to see Kellen and I embracing each other. I pulled back to talk to her, but he still held on like he didn't want to let me go after the moment we'd shared.

"I'm not even gonna ask," Lena said about seeing that we were back on good terms so quickly. "Wendy, Jimmy said get your black ass back on the floor or clock out."

"You want to tell her or should I?" Kellen asked with a smirk since we were the only two privy to my new secret and by proxy ownership.

"I'll do it. Lena, I'll explain everything later, but pretty much the diner belongs to me now and effective immediately you're my new manager."

"Kellen, I know you did not just buy my cousin this diner!" she exclaimed excitedly after putting the pieces together on her own like she was Sherlock Homegirl.

"He did. And you go tell Jimmy I said to take anything he doesn't want thrown away out of *my* new office before he leaves for vacation. And throw in that it's not personal, it's just business," I said wishing that I could personally get my lick back, but I didn't see myself leaving Kellen's side just yet.

Meanwhile Lena skipped off like a kid given permission to curse for the first time and I laughed what little ass I had on me off.

"You look like you really enjoyed doing that," he said looking down on me with that wide smile I had come to love.

"Because I did! I always thought I would be humble with 'fuck you' money, but apparently there's a new Wendy in town!" I joked even though I still felt like I would wake up any minute now. But if it did end up being a dream then I knew for sure that I wanted to finally at least make it one to remember. "Get up. Let's go."

"Where? It's coming down pretty bad out there," he said as he slowly stood, but I didn't have an answer because I hadn't thought that far ahead yet. I just knew that it should be somewhere close and private where we couldn't be interrupted.

"Um I guess up to my apartment then."

ALL YOU CAN EAT
AUGUST 19ᵀᴴ
8

The apartment above the diner had never been anything to write home about, but it was actually much bigger than people would have probably expected from the outside. It felt more like a shoebox then though with a tallish, dark and handsome man in it for the first time. Especially with us trying to keep our distance and pretending that we weren't there to have sex.

After climbing the flight and a half of stairs to get inside, Kellen was a little winded so I went to get him water while he caught his breath on the couch.

"It looks just like I thought it would up here," he said before taking a long sip from the glass and continuing to let his eyes take everything in. "Cute and tiny. Just like you."

I gave him a small smile as a thank you, but I was finally over all the small talk we had been doing for months. I was feeling bolder than I ever had been before and even though that still wasn't saying much I was sure that it wouldn't take too much convincing to get Kellen Turner into my bed.

"Is it just me or do you all of a sudden feel like we're stuck in a really bad Harlequin novel too?" I asked being about as subtle as a brick through a window.

"Why do you say that?"

"Because…it's all dark and rainy outside and you just revealed your big secret to me and saved the diner. So now the only thing left to do is…to *do it*."

"Well what happened to taking things slowly?" he teased me, but I noticed that was when he decided to finish his water then sit the glass down for good. Like he knew he should hydrate before what was coming next.

"I mean we definitely still can if you want to."

"Mm mn. I like the Harlequin idea. Go back to that," he said as he used his long arms to reach out and bring me over to stand in front of him. It felt like they could wrap around me twice as he quickly used them to untie my apron and server's pouch from behind my back.

My mind hadn't fully grasped that he'd already eagerly undid the buttons on my shirt until he got to the last one then suddenly stopped. We were just about eye to eye then so when he decided to look directly into mine, I could tell it really meant something.

"You're not just doing this because I told you I'm dying, right? I mean I'm not ungrateful and I'll happily accept pity sex from you, but I would love it even more if you do it just because you want it as bad as I do."

His nervousness was undeniable and it oddly put mine at ease because I realized that we were finally on the same page at the same time. I brought his big head down so I could kiss the top of it as he squeezed me in closer. I had been wrong before—being in his arms felt even more like home than connecting with his lips did.

"Kellen, I've literally been thinking about doing this since the first time I talked to your sad and sexy behind."

"You mean you knew you wanted me that first night too?" he asked as he gestured towards my hair asking if he could take it down. I undid the bun for him, but he shook it loose himself and got his fingers tangled in my woolly curls.

"Yeah kinda. Like I was obviously attracted to you, but I thought you were out of my league so I didn't put much thought into it until you asked me out."

"Now that's funny because I remember thinking the same thing which is why it took me a minute to even ask you," he said then grinned at my confusion as he kissed me again. "That right there. I didn't understand how you didn't know, but after I realized it I wanted to be the one to show you."

"Know what? Show me what?" I asked even more perplexed than before because he was making me think when all I wanted to do was feel.

"How beautiful and sexy you are," he complimented as he ran both hands up my thighs and under my skirt to take a peek at my panties like they were something he'd been curious about.

"Is this what you always wear underneath?" he asked about the lacy black bra and panties.

"Not even close," I laughed out because it was usually big ol' granny panties, but with laundry day approaching all I had left was the good stuff.

By that point my nipples were stiff and practically begging to be released, but he chose to let them stay captive and instead kissed and sucked on them through the fabric. The thin material might as well have been removed though since it did nothing to protect me from the heat of his mouth or the way he used his teeth and tongue to apply gentle pressure to them.

It almost felt like betrayal when he finally took his lips off of me, but I shivered down to my bones when I felt his hand part my thighs and graze my clit with his fingertips. That was when I knew I had misplaced my ever-loving mind because I did the unimaginable and literally begged that man to stop teasing me and get those clothes off my body.

"Alright. Alright, but before we start I just want you to know that we're gonna have to take this a little slower than you're probably used to."

"How slow?" I asked impatiently as I began undressing myself since he was still yapping instead of stripping me down.

"Slow. But with me slow doesn't have to mean boring," he said teasingly as he helped me take off my top then step out of my skirt. "And if you really need some speed I promise that my tongue can still go as fast as you want it to."

And I never make a promise that I can't keep!

"Look just put the condom on already because you talking to me like this is just torture at this point," I said playfully as I reached to unhook my bra, but I stopped when I noticed him suddenly looking unsure as he went to search his wallet then pockets.

"So about that condom…?" he began, but I didn't even let him get his thought out because we definitely needed one. "Right. It'd be a shame to get the clap on top of everything else I have going on," he cracked, but I didn't laugh so he made sure to clean it up. "Not that I think you have anything."

"Good because I don't have anything."

"Neither do I. Well I don't have anything *else*," he said as he held his chest, finally managing to get another chuckle out of me. I thought it was cute how he suddenly turned into a comedian when he was nervous.

"Will you shut up already? Now is not the time for jokes. We are here to have really good, no really great sex," I told him as I pried his hands off of me so that I could go ransack my bathroom for a condom that I knew I probably didn't have.

A few minutes of searching my medicine cabinet then under sink storage almost had me ready to give up until I spotted the gilded edges of wrappers sticking out from underneath a pair of flatirons I hadn't used in ages. I didn't know how or why a pack of condoms had managed to land itself there of all places, but it was none of my concern as I tried to keep myself from running back into Kellen's waiting arms.

I've got a golden ticket!

He had been taking his time thus far so I expected to find him still patiently seated on the couch, but instead he was relieving himself of his last piece of clothing which left him as naked as the day he was born. And as I slowly approached him again I swore that death had never looked so damn good.

Even with the little bloating he was still sculpted and built well and there was nothing boyish about his body. But the real star of the show resided below his waist and I mean it was just breathtaking—evenly-toned, veiny, and slightly curved like Captain Hook with a perfectly thick mushroom head.

"Alright before you say it, I already know what you're thinking," he began when he realized that my eyes were fixed on that part of him. "It's a shame it's gonna be six feet under soon, right?"

Like a dork I snorted and almost hit his chest laughing before I remembered it was probably sensitive enough.

"Why would you joke about a thing like that?" I asked even though I did agree with the sentiment.

"What? The only good part about dying is that now I can make inappropriate jokes about dying."

"Well make them some other time," I demanded before finding out just how warm his beautiful skin felt underneath my lips. His entire body suddenly caught a chill though as I kissed all of his scars and the evidence of treatment on his chest.

After finally ridding me of my bra and panties, we closed the small space between us until our naked flesh could kiss. His hands got back acquainted with my behind as he formally introduced his mouth to my bare breasts for as long as I could stand it, which wasn't very long, before I inched us backwards over to my room.

I cursed myself for being too lazy to make the bed before leaving for my meeting earlier, but I doubted that he even noticed or cared since his only concern seemed to be laying me back on it.

Before I could begin to prepare myself for what was coming, he'd already sandwiched his head between my open legs then buried his nose into my short, manicured hair. His body's reaction as he took in my scent for the first time was a sight to see and despite personally serving him meals for months I would have sworn he'd never eaten a day in his life.

Someday I would have to let Jenna know what had finally done the trick at getting his appetite back.

In the spot right above where he stirred his coffee, he used his tongue to stir my body only I didn't need any cream and sugar. Long seconds turned to minutes of listening to his satisfied slurps and moans until I almost thought I would never hear him speak again, but he decided to come up for air to make one request.

"Put your hands on the back of my head and hold it there. That's how I imagined it," he said with his eyes intently focused on mine before gripping my clit between his lips and immediately sucking the proud bud into submission again.

I did my best to comply, but it was hard knowing that he'd wanted me so badly that he had practically willed himself into me. It was almost too much to handle. My skin was on fire all of a sudden and I felt overwhelmed by everything all at once. Something powerful was building inside of me and I knew I wasn't ready for a release that strong.

"Hold on. W-wait a second," I begged him as I pushed his head away from me. I could tell he was confused since I had obviously been enjoying myself so while we both caught our breaths I tried to explain why I preferred not to reach my peak.

I told him how I really liked the intimacy of sex, the touching and rubbing, but that orgasms had always been a tricky thing for me. I could do a mild one with no problem, but I tried to avoid the ones that left me shaking and feeling like I was no longer in control of my body.

It was about as much as I could reveal without letting him know that I was actually full on crazy and that I couldn't even have better than average sex without experiencing anxiety. Luckily he nodded like he understood as he got up then lied down next to me. I still had an inkling that I had freaked him out some though until I saw his pearly whites in the dimly lit room.

"What are you smiling so big at?" I asked as I wiped his wet mouth with the back of my hand.

"Nothing. Just that I might be dying, but I still got it," he said mannishly as he licked his lips. I couldn't even deny it either because another minute of him down there definitely would have had me in a frenzied state.

He sweetly kissed my shoulder before asking if I wanted to keep going or not. I assured him that I did before handing him the condom, but he insisted on letting me do the honors.

I loved the way he felt in my hands and he was thick and juicy enough to play with for hours, but that would have to wait because at the moment we were both just anxious to finally get him inside of me.

"Don't be scared to tell me if you need me to stop again, okay?" he reminded me while positioning himself on top of me.

I nodded even though I knew I would be fine since I had never been able to finish from penetration alone before. I mainly just used intercourse to feel closer and connected to a partner.

Even through my half-lidded eyes I could see that his were wide open and studying my every move like a book. It wouldn't have been so bad if we were completely in the dark, but the fact that we weren't made it all the more noticeable.

"Um Kellen this is really…intimate," I said awkwardly and we shared a laugh.

"My fault. I just want to remember everything about this."

"No it's okay. I want to remember too. Just…" I said before bringing his head down to mine so that I could kiss his lips instead.

Much better!

The sudden invasion of his rigid warmth had been more than welcomed, but I still had to nearly gnaw on my bottom lip at the way he stretched me to my limits. Knowing that he could do serious damage if he weren't careful, he had thankfully slowly pushed his way in then let me get used to the fullness.

When his lower half finally came to life I already knew to expect a slower speed, but what I hadn't anticipated was just how rewarding the change of pace could be. I had long grown tired of being jackhammered anyway, but the way he seemed to tease me in calculated circles was something a girl could definitely get used to.

"That feel good to you too?" he moaned out then actually waited for my positive response before continuing.

I could tell he wasn't just asking as an ego stroke too. He genuinely just wanted to make sure

I enjoyed myself as much as he did. It was my first sexual experience where I felt like we were both present and in the moment. And what made it all the better was knowing that he wasn't fantasizing about somebody else because for whatever strange reason I was his dream woman.

I was especially impressed by how well his weak body had found the strength it needed to please mine. I felt the intensity building within me again when he started talking to me. I had gotten used to a little dirty talk from men over the years but never like him because his came with a side of affirmations.

Over and over again he told me how beautiful and amazing I was while giving me slow but powerful and precise blows to my core. I was so thankful that I had found those condoms because Kellen had planted himself so deeply in my rich soil that without one I would have surely been fertilized and full of his seed by that point.

I knew he was on a path to exploding because his mouth hung open as he went much faster than he probably should have been. But oddly enough I felt myself about to finish with him. My body felt engulfed in flames with each teasing stroke and the agonizing wait until the next one. I desperately clung to him, scared to feel what was about to happen to me but even more afraid for it to be over.

"Tell me to stop!" he begged in my ear since he had obviously felt the same wave of pleasure that had washed over me. All I could do was hold onto him though because I wasn't strong enough to fight the feeling anymore.

"That's right, you can't, can you? Because you deserve this shit. You're always serving. Now it's your turn. It's yours. Take it!" he grunted with his lips beside my ear.

My skin was hot and my anxiety was at an all-time high, but I just had to go with it because what other choice did I really have?

"Let it go, Wendy. I got you. You can let go with me. You can do it. I feel it. You're almost there. Keep going," he encouraged breathlessly like he was my coach and I was his star player.

He was suddenly forced out of me by all the pressure but quickly pushed himself back in and kept stroking me through his own closing moments. Hearing him loudly grunt and sputter until completion was like music to my ears and his trembling body only helped add to my sexual delusions of grandeur.

If I had been reading about the experience in a book I would have rolled my eyes so damn hard about us conveniently finishing at the same time, but I was so out of my mind then I didn't know what to do. I felt so disconnected from my body that for a while I thought the wheezing and heavy breathing was coming from Kellen until I saw that it wasn't.

My orgasm had nearly caused me to black out and a part of me really wished that it would have after seeing his scared face because that was when I felt the urgency, the sudden need to panic.

Logically I knew I was fine. There was no reason to fight or flight, but I still couldn't get my body to relax at will. The racing heart. The hot tingling skin. The loss of breath. My mind had interpreted it all as a panic attack and followed suit the same as it'd done earlier in the diner.

"Hey! Hey! Are you okay? Do you have asthma? Where's your inhaler?" he asked as he frantically got off the bed to search for it.

"No it's just…um…uh…a panic attack. I have them sometimes when I'm--when I'm--" I barely got out because I was hyperventilating so badly.

"Okay don't talk then. Just breathe and get grounded by looking at me," he said sounding like he was familiar with them as he put hands on both sides of my face and forced eye contact.

"Breathe with me, Wendy. I promise everything is alright and whatever you're worrying about, it's gonna be okay. Remember when you told me that?" he asked and I nodded so hard our noses collided.

"Say it…again please."

He let go of my face to get back into bed and hold onto me from behind as he repeated the words until he had synced his breathing with mine. It took a while, but my body slowly returned to its regular resting rate.

We weren't facing one another any longer because I was safely enveloped in his arms, but I still felt scared that I had scared him so I knew I needed to explain myself.

"I'm sorry. I don't do too good with my emotions sometimes and I just kind of tuck them away so when I'm under a lot of stress I have really intense panic attacks. Sex kind of does the same thing when it's good like that so you can at least take a bow," I said sarcastically and he lightly chuckled.

"It's okay. You don't have to apologize," he said as he pulled me closer then kissed the side of my head.

"Yes I do. I know you wanted a fantasy for your last hurrah not a headcase."

"No. I wanted you, Wendy. Just you. And you're not a headcase," he said as he gently moved hair out of the way to get a better view of my eyes. That led to him rubbing my scalp until his fingers got stuck in a mass of tangled sweaty curls.

"See that's why you're not supposed to play with it."

"Says who? I've been wanting to see it like this for a while. Like I'm seeing the rest of you."

"Naked?" I asked trying to lighten things up some.

"Unrestricted. I can't wait to tell Wendell and Ella that they really weren't messing around down here when they made you," he said intending it to be a compliment, but instead hearing my father's name when I was already feeling vulnerable had just made me catch a chill and tense back up.

"My fault. I didn't know that was a sore spot for you," he said sincerely before I unconvincingly assured him that it wasn't. "It's okay. We don't have to talk about it right now. Whenever you're ready."

I thanked him for the offer even though I was sure I would never actually need it, but something must've happened from the time he released me so we could go freshen up in the bathroom and the time we were back in my room.

"He used to hit her," I said directly into his chest since he had instantly gone back into holding me mode when we were back in the bed.

"Well that's putting it lightly. He used to beat the shit out of her right in front of me then get upset when I was scared of him. He never even gave her a chance. If she did something right or wrong. If she woke him up for work or if she didn't. No matter what he would always find a reason to go after her. My therapist says that's where my problems with anxiety started."

And to be honest I didn't think I would ever not feel like a failure for still not being healed from my earliest traumas, but it sure as hell felt good to finally say all of that to somebody who wasn't getting paid to listen to me. His response somehow felt even better though.

"I'm sorry," he said as he used his free hand to rub my back. I closed my eyes and enjoyed it until he asked the same follow-up question as every therapist I'd been to.

"No he never hit me. Maybe he would have eventually, but she got me out of there before it could ever happen."

"Do you know what finally made her leave?" he asked softly. I nodded as an errant tear fell which was weird because I didn't even remember feeling any building up.

"It was me. One day he punched her because he said she was ironing his work shirt wrong. She lost control of the iron and I swear the tip of it must've touched me for like a split second." I turned to show him the small scar on the apple of my cheek.

"But that was enough for her. When he left for work that night, she packed everything she could hold in one hand because she was carrying me with the other. And I was maybe five or six then so I was big enough to walk on my own, but she wouldn't put me down until we got here."

"Here?" he asked in surprise as he looked around my room and I smiled.

"Yeah. This was home for a while, but I don't remember any of it. Probably because we didn't stay long."

"What do you think she would say now that it's home for you again?"

"Well first she would ask about the naked man in my bed," I said being silly to give us a well-needed laugh. "But then she would tell me that she's proud of me. She always was. Even when I brought home mostly Cs she was still always so proud."

"Who wouldn't be proud of you? If I ever had a daughter I would've wanted her to be just like you. You're sweet and disciplined and you make men wait half a year just to get a date out of you," he joked.

"You regret not having any kids?" I asked when I realized how he had worded things.

"No. I've always wanted them, but I would've regretted having them more now that I'm not gonna be around."

"That's understandable. And sorry again for making everything about me today. You're the one *really* going through something right now."

"I think we both needed to share today. My mom used to say that shared pain is halved and shared joy is doubled."

"I like that. I think I'll start saying that too," I said before playfully acting like I was stealing the words from his mouth which made him smile.

"You alright now?" he asked through a contagious yawn. "Good because I feel like I just ran a marathon and I don't know how much longer I can stay up."

I laughed then gave him permission to roll over and go to sleep. I stayed up a little while longer thinking about everything that'd happened throughout the day, but since I had run the same race as Kellen sleep wasn't too far behind for me either.

We were both more tired than we had given ourselves credit for because over the rest of the day we would both wake up for a little while to talk and kiss for a few minutes before ultimately falling back asleep. I never wanted to leave this bed, but as much as my heart felt like I could survive off of him and only him around midnight my stomach said otherwise.

"I'm really hungry," he said beating me to the punch before kissing my shoulder to wake me up.

"Same, but I basically have nothing here."

"Can't we just get something from down in the diner?" he asked like it wasn't closed for the night.

Just when I was about to suggest something else I remembered that not only did I already have the keys, but I literally owned the place and I could do whatever I wanted!

I'd figured that we would both take separate but equally quick showers before heading down since my small bathroom was obviously not intended for more than one person. But Kellen had other plans and made it work after claiming to be an expert at making himself fit in tight spaces.

Eager to eat he'd quickly jumped back into his sweats after drying off, but when I grabbed something comfortable of my own to throw on he stopped me and suggested that I put my uniform back on instead.

"No panties," he further instructed as he pocketed the remaining two condoms out of the three pack so I knew he meant business.

"I always knew you had a little waitress fetish," I told him as I slipped back into the pink skirt and top then put my hair up.

To the naked eye I probably looked ready for work as usual, but my naked body underneath told a different story.

"More like a *you* fetish," he mumbled to himself on our way out.

The diner always looked pretty different with no customers inside, but that night it practically felt deserted since there were barely any cars on the road thanks to the rain still coming down outside.

Kellen finally got his full tour of the kitchen before we used leftover ingredients to make a couple of omelets and home fries. It was obvious that neither one of us knew what we were doing with the big cooktop grill, but it was still fun figuring it out together and luckily everything tasted much better than it looked.

Despite how good the meal was though neither one of us managed to clean our plates. Personally I had made sure to save room for something sweet because even though the sign on the door said *Closed*, I was still very much open for business and ready to play.

I left Kellen in the booth watching my every move as I walked over to the stool closest to the door then presented my backside to him like it was dessert.

"You're my last customer of the night, Mr. Turner so I sure hope I earned a nice big tip," I said trying but failing not to laugh at how unoriginal I must have sounded.

"After service like that you're about to get everything I got on me," he played along as he abandoned the booth then came over to me. "Get up on your knees."

I did as I was told and got on all fours with my hands firmly planted on the counter next to the register and tip jar. I was glad the crew had cleaned the area well for closing because I had a feeling my face would be on it in no time.

As he was preparing himself to safely enter me again I looked around in full disbelief of what was taking place. I was literally the last person anybody would have expected to buss it open in the diner yet there I was open and ready to receive. Because he had definitely been right about that—I deserved this.

"I really didn't think you had this in you, Wendy," he whispered proudly in my ear from behind as he sank himself back into me.

That's because I didn't. You brought it out.

"I'm full of surprises," I moaned out trying to sound like it wasn't my first time at the rodeo although it very much was.

"Actually you're full of me," he corrected as he started giving me all that I could handle and then some.

The fact that we were in the diner and out in the open seemed to add another layer of excitement for him this time around. He was even louder than he had been up in my room and I felt his legs trembling much sooner than before. But thankfully he was a gentleman in and out of bed I noted as he did a superb job of steadying himself to make sure he didn't finish before I did.

I knew it was game over for me though when he got talkative again. That was when my knees buckled underneath me and him hitting my spot became detrimental to my sense of balance. He held me in place for safety reasons of course but also so that he could finally let go and succumb to his needs.

Saying that we had merely satisfied each other would have been the understatement of the century. By the time we'd finished our clothes were in disarray, we had tipped over the tip jar and I knew for sure that I would never be able to use the register without blushing again.

"You good?" he asked after hearing me try to regulate my breathing before it got out of control again. I nodded and had barely come down from the high when I noticed him looking at the clock on the wall in front of us.

"Damn I really wasn't expecting to be out this late. I've got to get home."

Could you at least wait until you're not still inside of me to ruin things?

"Oh okay," I said trying not to sound disappointed because I had wrongly assumed he would be staying the night with me.

"It's just to get my medicine then I'll come right back, alright?" he yawned out as he bent to kiss the side of my face and neck.

"No, it's late and I can see you're tired. We'll just talk tomorrow."

"Yeah I guess we could do that…or you could always come with me."

I'd been curious to see how he lived since forever so in record time I packed a bag, checked on anything that could start a fire thrice and then we were off.

It was a no brainer that Kellen would have a nice place, but upon arrival at Lake Point Tower I knew that the word nice couldn't do it justice. We were practically steps away from Navy Pier and the lobby looked even more luxurious than it probably costed.

Despite how much work I had put into making it feel like home, I instantly felt ashamed of the little shoe box apartment we had just come from. I mean he'd only had five more years on earth than I did, but what he had done with it was remarkable.

Stop comparing yourself to others.

It was hard not to though after seeing signs with business hours for a restaurant, a spa, two pools and a convenience store all located on site.

I turned to him when we were alone in the elevator because I didn't have a very good poker face so I knew he could see the wonder in my eyes.

"You have a convenience store in your building."

"Yeah for convenience," he teased me before letting me know that there was also a whole Bean coffee shop on the ground floor where he got breakfast before finding the diner.

None of it seemed like a big deal to him though and that was when I remembered that he had grown up privileged too. Even still walking into his place was next level.

There was custom interesting modern furniture pieces that I assumed were made by him everywhere. I felt like I had stepped into a more stylish, Black bachelor version of *The Jetsons*.

He encouraged me to look around and make myself at home as he grunted and headed over to his room. He had clearly overdone things tonight but was still putting on a brave face for me. He was beyond exhausted and really needed to get some rest soon.

"You okay?" I asked following after him to get a good look in there first since I knew we wouldn't be up too much longer.

It was a big room expensively decorated in dark blues and blacks reminding me of the suits that he wore so well. An unlit fireplace sat in the center and made me imagine a romantic setup just like the ones in all the cheesy books I had devoured over the years.

"Yeah just gotta wait for these to kick in," he said before throwing back a handful of pills from his nightstand. "Do you have a favorite side of the bed?" he asked out of the blue clearly trying to change the subject.

"Not really. I took the left before, but I pretty much just roll all over."

"Good because I want to feel your head on my chest for a little while before we go to sleep."

"Listen you bought me a diner and you gave me a couple explosive orgasms tonight. You can have whatever you like," I sang the lyrics just like TI did which made him grin.

I left him to rest while I went from room to room nosily and noisily checking everything out. The bathrooms were gorgeous, the kitchen was a home chef's dream, but my favorite part was seeing the breathtaking view of Lake Michigan and the Centennial Ferris wheel from his balcony. I had a fuzzy memory of being at the top of the old one as a kid but no other details came to mind.

"You actually have a robot mop! Why did I think I was moving on up by finally retiring the bucket and getting a Swifter?" I joked and my heart smiled at the weak smile he gave me as I came back into his room.

Is this our room now?

"So all of this is really mine now?"

He nodded as I slowly walked towards him to finally get into bed for the night.

"And what about you, Mr. Turner? Are you all mine too?" I asked only because I didn't want him to think it was all about the material stuff with me. I honestly considered that part as a bonus since he had proven to be quite the treat on his own.

Before answering the question, he used his phone to turn off all of the lights then made sure that I was snug as a bug in his arms.

"'Til death do us part."

A LA CARTE
AUGUST 20ᵀᴴ - AUGUST 25ᵀᴴ
9

Not that I'd tried to stop him from doing it because I certainly did not, but it really was all Kellen's idea to officially take leave from work indefinitely. He claimed that he had been considering making the move anyway before everything had happened between us, but ultimately I knew where the truth lied.

He didn't have the strength to do both his job *and* me so one had to go…and it wasn't gonna be me.

It'd been a long while since I was in that stage where you had so much sex you thought you might die from exhaustion. And since Kellen really was in a position to do so, we had to be extra careful. I let him rest as much as possible and volunteered as tribute to get on top most of the time, but he didn't seem to care one way or another. Each time he just looked at me like he still couldn't even believe it was happening.

In between all the sex and the sleep we did somehow manage to squeeze in some talking to balance things out, but getting out all of that pent up sexual tension was definitely still priority number one. And considering his condition we both thought that he would be the more exhausted of us, but as it had turned out I really needed the break for rest too.

Usually I talked to Lena every single day, but being wrapped up in Kellen's good sheets had become my new full-time job causing me to unintentionally neglect her. That was why when I finally managed to get up before him at a decent hour, I snuck away to the bathroom to finally hear her voice again since she'd been kept up to speed through text messages.

"How's it going? How is he? How are *you*?" she fired off just above a whisper since she was probably still in bed next to Greg.

"He's fine. Sleeping right now. And as for me…well aside from the rug burns on my nipples, I guess I'm fine too," I told her as I adjusted them because they had been painfully rubbing against my shirts ever since we'd done it on the floor the other day.

"Wait how did you--ohhh. Okay Kellen! Let me find out dying dick is deadly for real," she teased me through a devious snicker.

"Stop. I already feel guilty enough like I'm taking advantage of him. He's so vulnerable right now."

"So? If you got rug burns on your titties that means he's enjoying himself so I say quit worrying and try to do the same. We both know how long you've been pining away for that man."

"That's the thing though. When I was fantasizing and pining I never thought it had an expiration date. It feels like I won the lottery but only because I'm about to lose somebody I care about. And we would have had a lot more time together if I didn't let my stupid list come between us."

"Nope. No list slander is allowed in my presence. I don't know another woman alive that could look a fine millionaire in the face and tell him 'I have to get right with myself before I make time for you'. Shit like that is unheard of and something to be proud of, Wendy."

Alright. Whatever. Yay me!

We talked a little while longer and tried to focus on literally anything other than the most recent events to no avail because this kind of stuff just did not happen to women like us. I had a windfall blowing my way soon and a new warm bed with a man in it who for whatever reason would do anything for me. I was blessed and intent on reminding myself of that as I climbed back into bed ready to anoint his awakening.

His back was still to me so I went to wrap my arms around him, but he had already been turning so that I could lay on his chest how he liked.

"She's right, you know?" he said in a clear voice unusual for when he was first waking up. I smiled wide because I could almost hear my mama saying that every closed eye wasn't asleep.

"You were being nosy?"

"Not on purpose. But I do want to hear more about all of the pining. You *pined* for me?" he asked with a smirk, but my meek nod just made him sigh. "We really need our asses kicked for waiting so damn long."

"Yeah and now it's too late."

"No. Even when I'm gone it still won't be over. I don't know where I'm going after this, but I plan on looking out for you from there too," he said like he actually had control over that sort of thing before leaning down to kiss my forehead and both cheeks.

"And I know it's a petty request, but promise me when you meet somebody else it won't be a customer from the diner," he said playfully, but I groaned out of frustration then pulled the blanket over my head.

"I don't even want to think about another man right now, Kellen. I just want you," I whined out as he released another heavy breath then pulled the covers back to see my face.

"I know. All I want is you too. It kinda feels like we've done this whole thing before, doesn't it? Maybe a few times or more."

"What do you mean? You believe in all of that soulmates and past lives stuff?" I asked surprised since I knew how much of his life was shaped by his love of all things science.

"I do now," he said simply before slowly sitting up then expounding. "There's no way that this is the first time I've loved you, Wendy. It happened too fast. It's weird like…like I already knew how it felt. I remembered and then my heart just automatically did it again."

He spoke in a far-off voice and I almost wasn't even sure he was talking to me until he began searching for clues on my face that I felt the same. And while I couldn't say for sure that I had picked up on any old memories from previous lifetimes, if reincarnation actually was real then I couldn't see how I would be able to forget the feelings that he'd been giving me because they were already going beyond our flesh.

Still all of that was minutiae compared to him just using the L word in our present lifetime with no hesitation, just letting it effortlessly roll off of his tongue. So of course I had to ask him to repeat himself.

"There's nothing wrong with your ears. You heard me. Now tell me you love me too," he gently demanded as he laid back down then put his lips within reach of mine. "Even if you don't really mean it. I just want to hear you say it."

"Well first, what's your definition of love?" I asked as a stalling tactic then watched as a few cute wrinkles formed in his forehead.

"I guess it's like feeling safe and in danger at the same time. Because you know that they could hurt you at any time, but if the love is real they would move mountains to make sure they didn't. At least that's how I feel about you," he said while maintaining sincere eye contact.

I inhaled deeply because I couldn't remember the last time I had told anybody those words let alone in a romantic way. They were a big deal for me, but hearing him speak that way made me more confident in exhaling then putting words to my feelings too.

"I love you too, Kellen."

"Damn you really said that like you meant it though," he joked making us both laugh. "Did you?"

"Did *you*?"

"You think I came to the diner every day for *like* and dry toast? It was always about loving you."

He was close enough for me to kiss without having to put a hand on the back of his neck, but I liked touching him there since we had been using it as a nonverbal way to let him know when I wanted him to head south. He immediately licked his lips like he could already taste me before sliding down the bed. I had a random thought when he took a pit stop to fondle my breasts though so I quickly brought his head back up.

"Kellen, what if some long-lost relative shows up and contests your will after you're gone?" I asked because it wasn't exactly like he was just leaving me some spare change. It was an amount that would have cousins he'd never heard of coming out of the woodwork for their piece of the pie.

"This isn't *Perry Mason* and I don't have any long-lost relatives," he informed me alongside a chuckle before reminding me that he and both his parents were only children. "But if you're really worried there is one thing we could do to prevent something like that."

"What is it?"

"You could always marry me," he suggested in his regular tone, but I laughed because I had been sure he was still kidding around.

"Wait you're serious? I'm sorry. I thought--"

"No I get it. You want a dream wedding someday with a man that you love."

"Kellen, if I married you it *would* be a dream wedding with a man that I love." I grabbed his neck for a real kiss that time to show him that I did in fact mean it. "I guess I just always imagined it would also be with somebody who would be here past our *I Do's*." He grinned at the thought.

"Yeah well better luck next time, kid because we're doing it. Better start looking for a dress too 'cause I already have a new tux," he said to my disapproving look like it would really just be that simple. "What? All we really need is an officiant and some flowers. It'll be like an episode of *Married At First Sight*."

"You watch that show?" I asked curiously because it was right up my alley but seemed out of character for him until I realized we hadn't even turned on a TV at all since I had been there.

"No. I mean sometimes if there's nothing else on I don't mind it playing in the background, but it's not something that I'm..." he said obviously lying before I interrupted him with the name of the most controversial cast member ever.

"It's on sight!" he threatened and we both exploded with laughter because it was the only acceptable response. "I would personally take him out for playing in that woman's face like that."

"Oh you mean the same way you played in my face when you ghosted me after our date?" I asked sarcastically then watched him wince like it hurt to even hear that he had hurt me.

"I'm sorry," he whispered apologetically against my lips then kissed lower promising to make it up to me, but I thought of one more thing I wanted to know before I would let him put us back to sleep.

"It's okay. I forgive you and I promise to marry you and never bring it up again if you can just be honest about something," I began, purposely setting the scene to sound serious when I was anything but. "Why don't you like being called Kel?"

The smile that took over his entire face made my heart and lower region jump with excitement, but I controlled myself as he sighed then finally explained another deep dark secret.

"Alright look I really planned on taking this to the grave and I was literally this close to it dying with me," he said playfully before I bit his peck for still making those kind of jokes.

"Ow! Okay. Okay. When I was younger everybody thought it was funny to say stuff like 'Hey Kel. Where's Kenan?' or they would put cans of orange soda next to me and ask me if I loved it," he grumbled out the last part and I screamed with laughter because I'd never made the connection to

Kenan & Kel even though I had loved the show on Nickelodeon as a kid.

"I'm sorry, but that is fucking hilarious," I said while trying to calm myself down, but I still had a case of the giggles especially when I asked him, "And do you by the way?"

"Do I what?"

"Do you love orange soda?" I barely got the words out before he was suddenly on top and tickling me all over.

"As a matter of fact I do! Everybody loves orange pop because it's fucking delicious! And thanks to people like you I can never drink it in public without feeling like somebody might put it all together," he said as I continued laughing uncontrollably at his tame version of childhood bullying.

After a minute we finally settled back down and he marveled over how fast my heart was still beating like it was something magical…and I guess it kind of was for somebody in his shoes.

"Yeah I could really use some of that these days," he said as he put my hand on top of his chest to really feel the drastic difference in speed.

"I've always wished I could slow it down some. It's not so much fun when I'm trying to sleep."

I reminded him of how he had been holding me whenever I woke up feeling anxious. And that was when he decided to remind me of how he preferred to distract me by finally ducking his head under the covers.

Another set of ruined sheets and a long nap later we were dressed in Kellen's jammies and ordering in for brunch. For days he had been saying that we had some serious things to talk about and I knew today was apparently the day when a man in a suit who I deduced was his lawyer dropped by with more paperwork.

He took me over to his modular coffee table and opened up a secret compartment underneath it that had a small hidden safe.

"What are you, El Chapo or something? There's not a gun in there is it?" I asked seriously but he just chuckled at me.

"You really watch too much TV. I'm just showing you where I keep a copy of the will and a few other documents," he said before pulling them out to go over a few important details with me.

Along with his will he had also made me his power of attorney and health so as unsettling as it must have been for him, we did have to discuss his final plans before it was too late. It seemed straightforward enough though and I assured him that I would do whatever he wanted until I actually saw the words in black and white on the page.

The first issue that arose was that he was adamant about not wanting to be resuscitated. I immediately let him know that I wasn't comfortable advocating for that because I believed in exhausting every possibility first.

"We've already done that. Anything else is just a temporary fix and just prolonging the inevitable," he said simply, but his somber words had the opposite effect on my ears and instead made them perk up.

"Well what is it and how long does it prolong things? Long enough for a transplant?"

"It depends, but again it doesn't matter. I'm not living in a hospital or wearing some jet pack looking thing just to keep waiting in vain."

"Why not? You're too cool for a jetpack? What, it's gonna clash with your shoes?" I asked hoping that he realized how superficial he sounded over something that could give him a chance to actually survive long enough to get a heart.

"No, it's because I would have to fully heal from an LVAD first so if a heart happened to become available around that time then I couldn't even get it," he said before closing the folder then sitting it in the open safe. "If it's meant for me then I'll get one. The end."

I meant to actually let that be the end since it was obviously his decision to make and he'd clearly made it, but I still had one last thing to say.

"I don't get it. You would rather just die than take a chance and sacrifice a little?"

"You're right," he said almost convincing me that I had gotten through to him until he went on, "You don't get it, Wendy and you never will. I'm tired of being poked, prodded and probed. And being told if I don't do this or don't do that then

I'm gonna die. It's like fuck it then. I'll just die because what am I really trying to live for anyway? To make more money? Or to-to--"

I didn't say a word to cut him off from speaking, but opening my arms for him had the same effect because he immediately stopped talking and accepted the embrace.

"It's okay to be scared."

"I'm not scared to die," he said muffled into my neck before I assured him that I believed him.

"I know. But I didn't mean scared to die, Kellen. I think more than anything you're scared to live. I just don't know why." He sighed deeply before letting me go so that we could look at one another again.

"Maybe because before all of this, before you, I wasn't always the best man that I could've been."

"And you're worried if you live longer that the new you won't stick around?" He nodded and I respected his honesty. "I wouldn't be too worried if I were you. You were patient with me even when you were running out of time. That says a lot more than you think."

I kissed his face for a while then went back into the files because I preferred to finish getting all of the grim stuff out of the way at once instead of spreading it out. Next up were his funeral plans, which seemed simple enough since he just wanted a viewing for his friends and employees to pay their respects.

"I would think somebody like you would want to be cremated."

"No. As a matter of fact I want you to make sure they super embalm me so when the zombies come back I can be the freshest corpse out here."

"Noted. Super embalming. Zombies." I pretended to jot it down before getting to the one thing I'd been curious about since he had first told me about all of this. "Should I be expecting any ex-girlfriends to show up?"

"Uh there might be one."

"The most recent one?" I asked as I brought his chin up to look at me since he had lowered it the second I brought up the topic. Expecting the worst I just asked the obvious, "What happened? What did you do to her?"

"Nothing. It was just kind of a convenient thing since we both worked a lot. I told her she didn't have to stick around for all of this and she didn't."

"So you basically gave her an out but didn't expect for her to actually take it?" I asked since there was a hint of sourness in his words. "Would you have done the same for her? Studies show most men leave when women get sick or hurt."

"I know, but I'm not them. I would never let anybody I care about go through this alone."

"Okay you're right. Enough with all the morbid talk today. Let's talk about something fun that you want to do before you're gone."

"I already did it. Actually I've been doing it a lot these last few days," he said before kissing my fingers then my bare shoulder where his silky pajama top had fallen from.

"I meant something that doesn't involve you being inside of me."

"Oh well then nope. I'm drawing a blank."

"Really? So your last plans are to just have sex until your heart finally gives out?" I asked seriously, but he confirmed it to be true when he laughed and nodded. "Kellen, that's not funny."

"What do you want me to say, go climb Mount Everest? I can't do anything. I'm actually not even supposed to be having sex."

"Yet you're still doing it every chance you get. Okay let's just go somewhere then so you can at least go out with a nonsexual bang. We could go tropical or historical or--"

"I'm not cleared to fly. I'm on standby so I have to stay within four hours of my hospital at all times," he said smugly before ultimately sighing at the circumstances. "It's fine. I already told you I'm not exactly a blaze of fire kind of person anyway."

"Well neither am I, but if I knew death was knocking on my door soon I'd like to think that it would ignite a fire in me," I said before wracking my brain for literally anything fun for us to do.

"See how depressing and limiting this is? That's why I would rather just stay here with you," he said as he pulled me on his lap then nuzzled my neck again. "Not just because it feels good but because it makes me feel normal."

I understood exactly what he'd meant because being with him had been making me feel the same way. It also made me want to ask about the kinds of things he'd done before being diagnosed.

I watched his eyes come close to glossing over as he reminisced about loving rollercoasters. He said he had always been thankful that he was on the taller side since it meant that he met height requirements before most other kids his age.

But he hadn't actually been on one since passing out on a ride on his senior trip in high school. At first his friends had laughed because they just thought he'd fainted from being scared, but really he'd gone into cardiac arrest.

"I coded at 18, but they were able to bring me back. Sometimes I think I wasn't really supposed to be here though."

"I think you were. For me. You keep getting a second chance because you're supposed to be here with me."

He nodded in agreement before leaning in to kiss my forehead. I knew it wasn't intentional on his part, but with his lips still on my temple it felt like he was kissing me with each word he spoke.

"I'm definitely glad that I got to meet you and experience you, but sometimes I miss how simple life was back when I was still that kid who just wanted to ride rollercoasters all day."

There were theme parks all across the state within a four-hour drive, but I knew that getting on any ride faster than a moving car was still out of the question for him. Still I could practically hear the nostalgic yearning in his voice and that gave me a different but safer and much closer idea that would hopefully give him the same kind of feeling.

"Get dressed. We're going out for a little while."

We literally hadn't left his place since we had gotten there days ago and we'd barely even been to the balcony so the hot sun felt good on my skin when we got outside.

"What are we doing here?" he asked me with a grin after the short Uber ride over to Navy Pier. I knew he couldn't do too much walking around so I'd decided to take him to the one place where we could get a little bit of everything in one spot.

"It's a surprise," I said hoping he hadn't already figured it out so quickly, but his expression said that he had.

"Are you really taking me on the Ferris Wheel? C'mon. It's like a rollercoaster for the terminally ill."

"Now why would I go and do something predictable like that?" I asked sarcastically hoping that he still liked it because it was the best I could do under the circumstances. "Will you still go on with me?"

"Yeah but only because you're even cuter when you're trying to be spontaneous."

We sat facing the lake so by the time we were halfway up in the air it looked like we were hanging above the water in the coolest way. I had read about the newer wheel being about fifty feet higher than the original one, but it felt like I could have reached out and touched the clouds in the sky if I wanted to.

Kellen was stiff in his seat and just taking it all in like he was seeing an old dear friend for the first time in years.

"You okay?" I asked with my hand on his chest to make sure that his breathing was stable since it looked like he'd been holding his breath.

"Yeah I'm good. It's just been a minute and…I guess I never thought I would get to see the world from up here again."

"You want to get off?" I barely got out before he was shaking his head and exhaling.

"No and we have to do this at least one more time before we leave," he said finally cracking a smile and sounding just as excited as I had hoped it'd make him feel. "Thank you."

After our third go-round I knew I had created a monster, but thankfully the pier closed at a decent hour otherwise he would have been on that thing all night long. And my goofy butt would have been sitting right there next to him the whole time because that's what you did when you really loved someone.

OPEN LATE

AUGUST 26TH - AUGUST 31ST

10

Before meeting Kellen Turner I'd had the simplest of nighttime routines. I would maybe spice things up occasionally with a facial after washing off the day and wrestling with my hair, but that was about as exciting as things ever got for me.

That simplicity had been nowhere to be found as of late though since every night before bed we *had* to get at least one Ferris Wheel ride in before heading over to the boat where we let the gentle waves of Lake Michigan rock us to sleep.

And again he had majorly undersold his "midrange cruiser" since the cabin literally had everything needed to live out on the water fulltime. If anybody had told me that this would be how I'd spend my two-week summer break from Jimmy's I would have laughed in their faces, but there I was loving every second of it.

To Kellen's dismay we had to give the boat a break for the night since the rain clouds had found themselves blanketing the sky yet again. I couldn't have been happier about it though since it meant I could finally get back to the fancy tub in the condo's master bathroom. I had never experienced jets hitting my back quite like that and with the way somebody liked to keep me lying on it I needed all the relaxation I could get.

I watched him dry off from his long shower, but I made no moves to finish up because the aforementioned jets were just beginning to really kiss my toes. He noticed and instead of rushing me to get out, he wrapped himself in a towel then just sat there and watched me enjoy it all.

Every part of my body was covered by bubbly suds so on the surface it was perfectly innocent, but the look in his eyes said that he couldn't wait to see me again when they popped.

"We really gotta get you thinking about something other than sex," I teased him before blowing a few bubbles in his direction.

"What's on your mind then?"

"Honestly things have been going so good that it's made me wonder what the hell you would've done to make us break up if you weren't dying." I was a natural cynic so I couldn't help it, but he nodded and took it in stride.

"Well you still haven't experienced one of my room-clearing farts yet, but aside from my bad gas my mom used to say that I was the most stubborn person she ever met."

I had obviously never met her, but I certainly agreed with the late Mrs. Turner since he had shut down every single attempt I'd made at getting him to consider the LVAD over the last few days.

"Personally I think my biggest flaw is that I drove past your diner every day for years and never thought to go inside until it was too late."

I could tell he was shifting into a more contemplative type of mood, but I didn't want to end such a good day on a sad note so I did what I knew would instantly cheer him up.

"Don't just sit there watching me like a pervert. You clearly want to get wet again so get in," I said suggestively as I sat up a bit to make room for him.

"I'm already dry, but I'll wait for you to come wet me up in the bed instead," he said not really paying me any attention as he checked the time on his watch. That was when I asked why he didn't remove it before showering because I knew it cost a fortune.

"It's waterproof," he said sounding like Mr. Moneybags as he finally got down on his knees and let his hand disappear under the suds.

My legs had already been open, but I put an arch in my back anticipating his long fingers finding their way home. Instead I got the loud sound of the doorbell ringing and startling us both into splashing each other.

"You ordered food?"

"Something better."

"What's better than food?" I asked sarcastically before he went ahead and dipped his fingers inside. "Mm. Don't be rude. Go answer first. I'll wait."

"They'll wait," he countered, but I clamped my legs shut until he did the right thing.

My nosiness kicked in the second he shut the door behind him. I quickly dried myself and slipped into his big fluffy robe, ready to ruin whatever surprise he had for me since none of mine ever went as planned.

The surprise had been on me though since it didn't dawn on me that whatever he was having delivered required an actual delivery person. But instead I and my half-opened robe delivered quite the view to the well-dressed older man while I was trying to sneak up on Kellen.

I quickly closed it before he could get a good look at my goods then gave an amused Kellen a dirty look since he'd thrown on a button-up and pants before letting the man inside.

"Beautiful jewels for a beautiful jewel," he said to me before politely speaking then turning back to Kellen. "You are a lucky man, Mr. Turner."

The kind words were put into better context when he stepped away from the luxurious display on the coffee table that hadn't been there before. The door closing behind him nearly startled me again as I had been put in a sudden trance by all the sparkling diamonds dancing in every direction.

"What's all of this?" I asked Kellen since even after blinking several times I just knew my lying eyes were playing tricks on me.

Because there was no way in hell that all of those assorted colors and different shapes were meant for *my* selection. I mean I knew nothing about diamonds and the closest I had even come to any were the cubic zirconia studs that I sometimes picked up at beauty supply stores.

Clearly amused at my stunned reaction, he reached out and pulled me over and onto his lap to get a closer look. He spoke through a grin and a kiss as he told me to get whatever I wanted.

"But they're all so pretty. How could I ever choose?"

"Who said you had to?" he asked simply enough like a heist's amount of jewelry wasn't the topic of discussion. "I told him we only needed to see rings, but he clearly knows a thing or two about upselling, huh?"

"And before you start worrying about the cost, don't because it's not anywhere close to how much you're worth to me. You deserve this and more," he remarked sweetly as he placed a heavy, ice-cold necklace on my collarbone.

I turned to admire it in the mirror beside us as he put a matching pair of teardrop earrings in my lobes. I then continued pretending like my hands didn't work and let him adorn both wrists with bracelets and place rings on all my fingers. There would literally never be an appropriate occasion that called for so much bling, but it was fun pretending to be royalty for a while the same way I had done when I was a kid.

"See how diamonds sparkle against skin like yours, Wendy? It's just different. I guess that's part of the reason why I've been imagining you in nothing but them for as long as I've known you," he said innocently enough, but I immediately knew what he wanted.

He had seen me naked countless times since our first time, but it was always in dim or dark lighting or just for a second before I got into bed. He wanted to finally *see* me though and I decided to let him since he had been the one to see a version of me that nobody else ever bothered to look for…and now I wanted to see it too.

I felt flutters in my stomach as I took my hair down from the towel, but there was a full-blown butterfly effect going on in there when I stood and let the robe fall from my bare shoulders down to my feet. His juicy bottom lip separated from the full top as his wide eyes appreciated his fantasy come true in the flesh.

My own lips quickly did the same because after admiring me from all angles he wasted no time letting his fingers invade then instantly conquer the most precious gem that I already owned. My legs naturally spread for him as my body accepted being simultaneously explored and ravaged beyond recognition.

By the time I could get my rolling eyes to sit in the front of my skull again I was literally springing a leak on his thrusting fingers, but even that didn't make him stop his erotic probe. The sleeve of his crisp white shirt had even come undone by then and was now transparent from being drenched with my appreciation. And I couldn't help but think that it really was a good thing that his watch had been waterproof after all.

"Damn. When's the last time you let somebody touch you like this?" he growled out as he peered up into my eyes.

I could barely hold onto his shoulders for balance and shuddered my way to completion as my breathing and emotions almost got the best of me. I did my best to focus on inhaling through my nose and exhaling through my mouth until I was coherent enough to answer him.

"Mm. Nobody but you has ever touched me like this," I confessed through a guttural moan as his mouth began making its way down to the priceless pearl between my legs.

SORRY FOR THE WAIT
SEPTEMBER 5TH
11

All the signs were there that Kellen and I wouldn't just be going down to the courthouse for a quick ceremony to validate our marriage license. He'd done the over-the-top gesture of showering me in jewels a few nights ago and he had been very secretive and more into his phone than usual.

The fact that it was Labor Day and the place wouldn't even be open should have been my biggest clue, but that literally didn't cross my mind until much later. We got up that morning, had a light breakfast then wound up back in bed like any other day, but as soon as the clock struck noon I realized that things would go a little differently than I'd assumed.

The doorbell hadn't jolted me awake from our afternoon nap because I'd already been up and feeling on Kellen who was pretending to be too tired for another round. Red flags should have been going off in every direction from that alone, but I had just gotten up to see who the hell was at the door interrupting my grinding.

Of course I would never have actually been rude to whoever was on the other side, but even the thought was absurd when I saw a squad, no a battalion of sturdy and stoic women in white standing in the hall.

"Um…hi. Can I help you?"

"Are you the bride?" the smallest but still very tall woman asked in a gruff voice revealing herself to be the leader of the pack.

"Kind of. I mean yes," I answered before realizing that it had to have been yet another surprise set up by Kellen.

I quickly welcomed them inside before excusing myself to go back to the bedroom for a minute where I found him lying with his hands behind his head like he was expecting me.

"Tell me you didn't really think I was gonna just take you to circuit court to get married."

"Not before you tell me you didn't really hire a team of scary women to beautify me for the day," I countered since I had seen all the supplies and equipment they'd brought along with them.

"Actually I hired them to pamper you because you're already beautiful. Now go let them get started. We gotta be out of here by five."

"And what are you gonna be doing while I'm getting pampered then?"

"First rest up for the honeymoon tonight," he said suggestively with a wink, "then I'll get a haircut later."

"Really? I was just starting to like the scruffy look on you," I teased him on my way out even though it did suit him just as well as his regular clean-cut look did.

"Don't forget to pick out a ring," he reminded me before rolling back over to get some more shuteye. I couldn't afford that luxury anymore though because the army of no limit soldiers in the living room were clearly ready to prepare me for war and then for my wedding.

They quickly set everything up in one of the spare rooms and for hours I was massaged and manicured then plucked and pedicured. There had already been a natural glow to my skin, but I was shiny like a new penny by the time they got done with me. I even felt brand new too only that might have had something to do with all the champagne they gave me.

When I finally got a good look at myself in the mirror I was thoroughly impressed with the woman looking back at me. I had never seen my makeup looking so natural before, not even when Lena had done it. It barely looked like I was wearing any and it gave off a flawless *I woke up like this* vibe.

They had tried over and over to get me to straighten my hair for the occasion, but with the way the sun had been coming in the windows and the way Kellen loved to make me sweat it would've been back in a fro in no time. Besides I couldn't remember the last time I'd seen a bride with an afro so I let my hair do its own thing.

It was silly of me to assume that my temporary ladies in waiting also had an assortment of wedding dresses for me to choose from, but I had done just that since they seemingly had everything else taken care of.

However, the one and only perfect dress for me could have only come from a more permanent and loving fixture in my life.

"It's sickening how much this man loves you, Wendy!" Lena exclaimed as she unzipped a bedazzled garment bag to reveal the dress she had chosen with me in mind.

I had been a little worried at first because it looked way too big and showed *a lot*, but she just told me to trust her and the process. I was glad that I had done that because after she'd finished pinning it in a few places the mermaid silhouette looked like it was invented just for me.

"You'll definitely need Kellen's help getting out of it, but at least it'll look good for the pictures," she told me as she hurried to put on a nice long dress of her own since apparently she knew more about my wedding day plans than I did.

"Um I don't think we're going to take any pictures. He's just doing all of this because he thinks it's what I want, but I doubt I'll actually want to remember this after…you know?"

It had been fun getting done up and doted on all afternoon long, but it wasn't until that very moment when it really hit me that I would actually be a widow soon. She must have seen the tears beginning to well in my eyes because she immediately started fanning my face at hurricane speeds.

"No crying! We're supposed to be happy! My girl went from no man and no money to married with millions real quick and I stan! Greg is forever popping vitamins and working out so messing around with him I'm never gonna be a fabulous rich widow!" she joked trying to appeal to my silly side, but it wasn't working today.

"I never thought I would say something like this, Lena, but I would give it all up for him. All of it."

"That's because you got used to being a broke bitch," she said making me unexpectedly spit with laughter. "I would trade Greg in for the boat alone. Period!" she claimed and we continued cackling like hens until there was a knock on the door.

It was Kellen poking his head in to tell us it was time to leave, but Lena quickly stood in front of me to block his view claiming it was bad luck to see me before the wedding.

"Bad luck like one of us might die soon or something?" he asked her sarcastically which made her gasp out loud because she didn't know how much he played around with the topic.

"Kellen stop. That's not funny," I whined trying to get a good look at his face, but Lena moved again to prevent him from seeing me.

"Alright I'm sorry. But just so you know hiding her is pointless because I've already seen all of her this morning, a couple times," he said making it sound so icky.

"Oh y'all are real nasty," she said as she grabbed her bag then left to touch up her makeup, allowing Kellen to get the first official look at his bride.

If he had been a cartoon character his eyes would have sprung straight from their sockets with how wide he'd opened them. I couldn't do anything but smile and also appreciate how good my groom-to-be looked in a tux with his fresh cut and shave.

"How did I get so damn lucky?" was all he managed to get out after admiring me for a full minute.

"Says the one who's dying."

"Yeah, but I get to make you Mrs. Turner first so it's all good. You'll finally be among the greats, not that there are many besides Tina and me of course. We can't even claim Ike for moral reasons," he joked getting me to crack a smile.

"What about Ted?" I asked naming the only other Turner that came to mind, but he instantly vetoed him for his lack of melanin. "Okay what about Nat then?"

"Brother Nat definitely counts," he joked as he bumped my fist with his. "You know if you do decide to use Turner now then your initials will go from W.E.B. to W.E.T. and I just want to say from experience that it's accurate as hell."

"Nope if you're just gonna be mannish and make death jokes then I'm gonna put you out."

"Fine, but first let me tell you how beautiful you look," he said probably because I had been fidgeting with the dress.

"Really? I don't feel like it."

I turned to get a back view of myself and scrunched up my face. No doubt it was a gorgeous look from top to bottom, but I still couldn't help thinking it would look even better on a taller or curvier body.

"You know you're really not supposed to date let alone get married when your self-esteem is so low, but lucky for you I won't be around long enough to take advantage of it."

"You wouldn't anyway. You're one of the good guys now. That and your money is why I'm marrying you today," I said sarcastically, but he frowned. I'd figured it was about the money comment until he explained.

"Before I go I want to do everything possible to make sure you see what I see when I look at you. You're good enough on a bad day, Wendy. Not that I would even know what that's like because I haven't had a bad day with you yet," he said genuinely as he lowered himself to get down on one knee.

"The ceremony is just a formality for the state. Marry me right here," he begged as he pulled out the gorgeous solitaire that I'd singled out from the bunch and left on his pillow while he slept.

And with a face full of makeup-ruining tears, I said yes.

I's married now!

The actual ceremony proved to be much more than a formality though and had been beautiful beyond belief. We didn't have to go far either since he had arranged to have it in Skyline Park which was on the street level to the tower.

The pond looked ethereal and the aisle I walked down was naturally bordered by so many flowers that it could have been mistaken for the garden of Eden. Aside from the familiar faces of my diner family and a few relatives I didn't recognize any of the many guests, but I just smiled and went with it since they all looked happy to see me.

By the time I finished meeting everybody who was anybody to Kellen I was starving and couldn't wait to get to our meal. I definitely got way too full though and had more than my share of drinks because I actually got courageous enough to dance in public. It was adorable seeing how much chemistry we had as a couple though since we hadn't even been together long.

Nobody expected the sudden venue change when the sun began to set, but for the first time ever Kellen couldn't get a surprise over on me. I knew he wouldn't even let the wedding stop him from his new favorite pastime, watching the sun slowly fall from the sky from the top of the city.

It was the perfect way to end the reception, all the people that had come out to celebrate with us on one magical rotation around the pier.

Kellen and I were both yawning getting into the Corvette to leave for our staycation honeymoon, but Lena wouldn't let us go without wishing us well and telling Kellen that just like her favorite actor Matt Damon he had now gotten married to his favorite waitress too.

That made me smile the entire drive over as I laid my tired head on his shoulder and tried not to focus too much on what the future held for us. I just wanted to pretend like we would be husband and wife forever.

"Did you like everything?" Kellen asked like the answer could be anything but yes as he carefully helped me out of the dress. I'd tried my best to remember where all the pins were and remove them myself, but after getting nicked a few times I gave up and asked for help.

He felt around for a while like he was reading braille then pulled out the last one in the back which made the whole thing fall to my feet. He looked surprised that I only had on a tiny pair of white panties underneath, but once it dawned on him he immediately tried to give me a few of his tired and tipsy kisses.

"Just go to bed man! You're so sleepy it's ridiculous!" I screamed out laughing as he scooped me up by the waist and made me wrap my legs around him.

"You know I can't go to bed until after we're done consummating this marriage. It's the rule."

"Kellen, there's no rule that says we have to have sex tonight."

"First of all it's literally the law and I'll be damned if I break the law for you, Wendy," he said being silly as he went to lower me on the bed.

"Okay, but at least come shower with me to wash off the day first," I said urging him to put me down, but he carried me over instead.

"We can definitely go get in the shower, but I'm never washing this day off of me," he said sounding so sweet that it along with the rest of the day had earned him an endless supply of some of the best honeymoon head imaginable.

The entire suite had been decorated really romantically, but nothing could have prepared me for all the greenery in the bathroom. I swore that I could feel the eucalyptus calming me the second we entered, but the most exquisite feature was hands down the ceiling mounted rainfall shower with LED lights.

There were no shower caps so my hair went just as unprotected under the downpour as Kellen had been when he glided into me with nothing between us for the first time. We had wanted to experience each other that way before it was too late so we'd done everything that needed to be done to make it happen responsibly.

Before Kellen I had never been much of a rider, but being with him brought out the confidence I'd always needed to do it well. As he sat comfortably on the white shower seat, I drove us both crazy with the chaos I was creating with my lower body.

Every time I got too eager and involuntarily sped up he would guide my hips and slow them back down. It was agonizing but so damned erotic how he was literally fucking patience into my body as we soul-stared and slowly grinded into one another.

If I hadn't been sure that we'd ever done it before, I knew for a fact then that we'd made love to one another as the balmy water rained down on us. Because it wasn't just about our bodies rubbing together and feeling good while we did it. We were healing and nourishing each other's spiritual wounds and exchanging loving energy in a way that I had never done with any other man.

Instead of trying to avoid the anxiety and mayhem that orgasms temporarily made my body experience, I embraced it and let myself pick up speed again. It must have felt just as amazing to Kellen because even though we both knew I was going too fast neither of us had the wherewithal to slow me down from that point forward.

Our sudden shared finale was unexpected, explosive and nearly catastrophic as we both desperately clenched and clung to each other trying to find a breath to breathe with the then intrusive water still coming down on us.

"I'm sorry! Shit!" I frantically apologized and tried to separate us when I noticed he was in pain and clutching his chest, but he just held me tighter with his other arm and refused to let go.

It took a long time for his breathing to stabilize again so I expected him to scold me for not controlling myself and putting him in danger, but instead he just looked impressed at what I had pulled out of him. Men really were a different type of animal.

SEPTEMBER 9TH

After nearly committing a honeymoon homicide on night one I was reluctant to go near Kellen again, but he didn't let me go more than twenty-four hours without convincing me that he was well enough to let me saddle up again.

We stayed at the hotel for a few days and pretended like we really were away somewhere on a tropical and exotic vacation. But in reality all we actually did was eat, have sex and catch up on the episodes of *Married At First Sight* that we'd missed because of our own television-show-worthy few weeks. Everything was perfect…until it wasn't.

We were back at home again when I realized that I hadn't seen Kellen use his phone the whole time we were away, a direct contrast to how he had been leading up to the wedding. I asked him about it right as we were getting into bed and watched as he snapped his fingers then pulled it out of the nightstand drawer.

The argument could have easily been avoided if I hadn't asked why it was in there and

179

not with the rest of our bags that we'd lazily left by the door, but it clearly needed to happen so I regretted nothing. I immediately took it from him to make sure that there were no missed calls from the transplant center.

I knew exactly which two numbers to look for since he had recently added me as his primary emergency contact although it wouldn't have been necessary to reach me in this instance since I would be the cause of the emergency.

"Look I can explain. It's not a big deal. I just wanted some time away from it so that we could enjoy ourselves and not have to think about any of this stuff, alright? I'm tired and I really don't want to fight about this," he said before bringing my palm up to his mouth as if that would be enough to stop my skin from smoldering from the inside out.

Molly, you in danger, girl!

I couldn't contain the rage I felt nor control my tongue any longer as I snatched my hand away from him then angrily threw the phone on his lap.

"No! You don't get to decide what we fight about. You're on standby! That means you also don't get to walk away from your phone ever let alone for days. You could have missed a heart, Kellen!" I yelled as I pushed the blankets off of me because I was so hot I felt myself beginning to sweat.

"Obviously I didn't or you would've said that!" he countered as he tossed his phone back on the stand and adjusted his pillow like I was actually about to let him sleep.

"Yeah but the point is you could have! First you refuse to get the LVAD and now you're even acting indifferent about a transplant? What is it with you? Why don't you want more time with me? What, a low-class waitress isn't good enough to be with unless you're fucking dying?"

From the way he sprang back up again I could tell that I'd surprised him with those words. And even though they had come from my mouth I couldn't believe that I'd finally said them out loud since they had been in the back of my mind all this time.

"Tell me you're just being dramatic right now because I know you can't really believe that after everything we've been through together."

"Why wouldn't I believe it? It's exactly what it looks like! Do you know how humiliating it was for me to meet your best friends for the first time at the wedding? I didn't even know their fucking names because you've kept me sequestered from your life like I'm on a jury or something!"

"Wendy, if I was ashamed of you we would have gotten married at the JOP with Lena as a witness. I wouldn't have rushed invitations to everybody in my rolodex just so they could see me happy one last time before I die with the only person who means anything to me!" he loudly proclaimed, but I was admittedly already too invested in the argument to really hear that part.

"I love you, okay? So why can't that just be enough for you?"

"Because you said when you love somebody you move mountains for them, but it's a lie because you won't even live for me!" I exclaimed as the first few tears broke through and cascaded down my cheeks.

"Okay and now you're the expert on love? How would you even know what love is when you've never let anybody close enough to actually fucking love you?" he spat angrily as he got up from the bed ready to leave the room, but my emotions were high so I was right there behind him to keep things going.

"Well unlike you I at least know it doesn't always look like picture perfect fucking health all the time!" I said to his back as I crashed into it since he had suddenly stopped walking in the hall.

I sniffled through more tears as he turned back around to face me. He bent to connect our foreheads as we took several deep breaths together and quickly decided to deescalate things before we said something worse that couldn't be taken back.

"You really love me, right?" I asked him softly, trying to clear away any hints of anger in my tone.

"More than anything. You have to believe me when I tell you that, Wendy. I wouldn't lie about that," he pleaded into my mouth as he kissed me and pressed his body into mine. I wasn't trying to have makeup sex just yet though.

"Okay then you're proving my point. There might not be something we can pinpoint on my body, but my mental health isn't exactly the best and you still love me anyway."

"That's completely different," he said dismissively as he let his hands fall from my body, but I picked them right back up and put them around me again.

"Why? Because when I wake up in the middle of the night you hold me just like this until I feel safe, right? You take care of me, Kellen, and I just want to do the same for you. I'm literally begging you to let me. I want to. Whatever it takes."

"No! You don't know what recovery looks like after a transplant. They tell you your life can eventually get back to the same, but it's a fucking lie. It'll just be more biopsies and pills and appointments and I don't want to be a patient anymore. I don't want you to have to become my damn caretaker. You have your own dreams and your own shit to worry about. I saw what this did to my parents' relationship before they died and I would never want to burden you with it."

"But you wouldn't be a burden!" I shouted at him again since saying the words more gently still didn't register with him.

"Yes I would! You've already waited on people for years now and I don't want you coming home and doing it for me too."

"Then we can hire people to help so it doesn't become too much for me."

"It's already too much. I can see what it's doing to you mentally now and I'm so fucking sorry. I should've never gotten you involved in this. I should've just left you alone and left the will like I always planned to."

"Well you didn't and I am involved now. And you're forgetting something really important in all of this. You weren't the only one waiting! And now that I have you I'm not just gonna let you go. I know this marriage is supposed to be about safekeeping the money, but more than I want an ironclad will I want you, Kellen. I want you for as long as possible. Can you please just consider it for me?" I begged him with everything I had inside of me, but it was all in vain since it was just met with yet another deep sigh.

"Wendy, I want you too. More than I could ever show you. But I want you to have the best version of me. Not this. I want to be able to make love to you in a body that's not so damn fragile."

"Oh please! This fragile body has given me the best sex I've ever had! And this version of you is the only one I know and the only one I want. I have the diner. I have money. I have everything I ever thought I wanted, but now it's not enough anymore because I want you too. And it's not fair for me to have to watch you slowly die when you have options."

"I know and again I'm sorry for that. I really am. But I'm never gonna change my mind about this. Sitting around and waiting for it to be over isn't fair to you either though so I promise I won't hold it against you if you want to go."

I already knew that leaving him was the last thing he wanted in the world, but the point was really driven home by the fact that he couldn't even look at me while he was saying it.

If I was being honest though I would have told him that he deserved to be alone until the end because it would be his karma for making me go the rest of my life without him. But bringing myself to deliver that level of truth was something that I just couldn't do to anybody let alone the man I loved.

"When did I say I wanted to leave?" I asked still attempting to hold onto my anger but letting our lips touch all the same since I was finally ready to release the recently accumulated tension.

There were equal amounts of fire and desire in his eyes and I felt the tingles in both of our bodies before I could even get my next words out.

"Death is the only thing that could ever keep me away from you again."

LAST CALL
SEPTEMBER 15TH - SEPTEMBER 19TH

12

The day it happened, the day that changed everything, it was like I'd already known that something wasn't right. Even excluding the fact that Kellen had spent all morning in bed so tired he could barely hold his head up, there was just something in the air.

After our long overdue argument the previous week we'd had a few more good days at home as man and wife, but the last couple had given me a glimpse into just how sick he actually was. His appetite vanished again, he went to sleep early and often and he didn't even want to go to the pier if by chance he was awake then.

The only good thing about him sleeping so much was that it gave me plenty of alone time to run the diner from home. Lena and I had been winging things so far since Jimmy hadn't left us any instructions nor had anybody in the family heard from him since he'd left for vacation.

"I see you're adapting to the role of boss without any issues," Kellen said startling me as he came into the living room. I had just ended a call and wasn't expecting him to be up for a while longer.

"Oh there have definitely been some issues. The guy that sells those big cheap wings to Jimmy was trying to make Lena sleep with him to get the same deal tomorrow. I tell you, birds of a feather."

"You need me to handle it?" he asked instantly going into protector mode even though he was wrapped in a blanket and still in his jammies well into the afternoon.

"I already did but thank you." I gave him a quick peck on the lips as he joined me on the couch, but he seemed to want more as he ran his hand up my thigh. "You finally get a teaspoon of energy for the first time in days and this is how you want to use it?"

"The fact that you even have to ask makes me think you don't really know me at all," he said playfully as he laid on his back then brought me along with him.

"I know you need to eat some real food before you even think about putting me in your mouth," I said sternly since he'd only nibbled on crackers for me a couple of times when I'd gotten worried.

Right when he was about to protest and claim he wasn't hungry we heard a series of beeps coming from somewhere. It almost sounded like the smoke detector so he got up to check the kitchen, but that was when I realized it had been coming from underneath him and a couch pillow.

It was my phone.

"Kellen, it's not the smoke detector," I said hurriedly before making the leap to the other side of the couch to answer the call in time.

"Your phone doesn't beep like that. Whose phone is that?" he asked curiously, but I was too busy fussing with the damn thing which was giving me a hard time swiping it.

Finally I got it open and it was exactly who it was supposed to be. I could hardly get the words out as I jumped up to hand him the phone.

"It's the transplant center. They're ready for you at the hospital!" I squealed excitedly then clamped a hand over my mouth so he could speak to them without any interruptions.

His hands slightly shook as he put the call on speaker then sat it on the coffee table so that I could listen in with him. He took a deep breath and closed his eyes before getting on the line.

"This is Kellen Turner speaking," he began before reaching over to grab my face and kiss me like it would be his last time despite what the woman on the line was about to tell him.

It had been a good thing that he already knew the drill too because with all the passion he used to kiss me and his big hands covering my ears, I'd missed some of the instructions. The second the call ended he fished out a prepacked duffel bag from his hall closet then sat it by the front door.

"I only gave them your number as a backup. I wonder why they called you before me," he said as he removed his pajamas then quickly got changed into comfortable clothes.

"They actually didn't. After you left your phone here while we were away, I had your calls from the center forwarded to me with a special tone just in case."

"You did that for me?" he asked like he was still surprised at how much I loved him too. He took a lip-biting step towards me like he was about to pounce then stopped himself. "You're lucky we have to go. Because if they would have called just a few minutes later I would be the deepest I've ever been in you right now."

My body tingled hearing him talk like that, but I knew we had no time to act on our desires so I brushed it off.

"Come on. We're focused on your heart right now, not your penis! Let's go, Turner!" I cheered when I realized that this was really happening out of nowhere. Lena hadn't been lying when she'd said that my manifestation skills were unmatched.

We held hands in the elevator as I talked him out of taking the Corvette because he wanted to *ride to the hospital in style*. I didn't know how to drive that thing though and I certainly wasn't letting him get behind the wheel now of all times so the sedan won no contest.

We were in the parking garage safely buckled up with my hands at ten and two when he grabbed the two hand and brought it up to his lips. Before I could turn to see him kiss it, I felt the sudden downpour from his eyes which let me know I needed to cut the engine for a second.

"I'm sorry for all of this. For not telling you everything from the beginning and for making you worry about me and the LVAD and just everything," he got out before finally breaking down and letting his proud shoulders shake and fall.

I had us out of our seatbelts in a jiffy and I was practically in the passenger seat with him doing my best to console him. It seemed like he really needed to just get it out though so I gave him space to do just that for a while.

"I know I must've really turned your world upside down when I came in it, but sometimes it feels like I didn't even have a world until I met you. I was alive, but I wasn't really living until you gave me a reason to."

We have something in common!

"I feel the exact same way. But we'll have plenty of time for proclamations of love and orange soda after we go get you a new heart, Kel," I teased him one last time just for the hell of it as I wiped his tears.

From the time we had gotten the call to the time we were signed in, just over thirty minutes had passed so we were more than on schedule for Kellen to get examined. But upon arrival that weird feeling I'd had all day suddenly came back when they told him that his regular specialist wouldn't be back in town for another day.

I tried to remain positive because they at least got her on the phone to advise, but again I just had a gut feeling that something was off and I had never wanted to be wrong so bad before. I sat and watched as patiently as possible as they ran countless tests on him to determine how well his other organs functioned as well as the more common blood tests.

I finally got to see exactly what he'd meant about being probed, but he endured it all with a strength that I admired since regular old pap smears always left me feeling uncomfortable.

After the testing stage was eventually completed the only thing left for us to do was wait, which was luckily an area we both had plenty of experience in. It was nerve-wracking at first but surprisingly not as bad as I thought it would be. I could tell he was nervous, but I had learned that that was precisely when he was at his funniest.

He made room for me in his bed and we managed to get a little shut eye in in between all the laughs. It was just after ten at night when I woke up to a calm Kellen lying beside me and aimlessly looking up but not quite at the ceiling.

"Don't panic, okay, but I think this might be a dry run. Organs are only viable for a certain amount of time and we're almost passed it." I didn't panic, but it did cause me to immediately sit up. "It's normal. Most people get called in a bunch of times before they finally get a good match."

"But why do they call y'all in unless they're sure it's a match?" I asked since it had to be unethical to keep getting peoples' hopes up just to let them down time after time.

"Because there are a lot of other factors that go into it besides just matching. There could be something they didn't see on the heart until the inspection or there might even be something else wrong with me," he said nonchalantly, but that was when my panic started slipping back in.

"Wrong like what? Is it my fault?"

"How would it be your fault?"

"Maybe because I've been fucking you to death for the past month."

"No, it's probably just a little infection. They'll give me some pills and we'll be out of here in no time. We get them sometimes from all kinds of stuff."

"Like licking me where I told you not to lick me?" I asked just above a whisper, but he laughed so hard he nearly coughed up a lung.

"Wendy I did not get an infection from eating your ass," he said still amused as I went to cover his loud ass-eating mouth.

"Do not say that in here!"

"So you'll let me do it a bunch of times, but I can't say it? And quit acting like you tried to stop me because it was definitely love at first lick," he said finally making me laugh right before we heard a team of people talking outside the door.

We instantly straightened up then kissed one last time because this was the moment we had been waiting for all day. The wait proved to be in vain though and the smile that had just appeared on my face fell the instant the doctors asked if we were familiar with the term dry run.

They went on to explain that while the donor heart seemed to be a good match on paper, upon further review the surgical team found that there was too much damage to transplant it. They apologized and said that they would give us time alone before explaining what would happen next.

I had been a silent but hurt and pissed off bystander until that last part because I knew there wasn't supposed to be anything happening next. This was the part where we were supposed to be going back home and praying for another call soon.

The other white coats left but one remained to deliver the knockout blow that Kellen actually wouldn't be going anywhere. The good news was that he didn't have an infection, but in layman's terms the rest of his body had been working much too hard to overcompensate for his heart.

Since he'd last been seen his condition had gotten increasingly worse and their call for him to take it easy to make the wait easier on his body had obviously been ignored. That part was like a dagger to my own heart to have confirmation that it was my fault too because I knew that us being so active was responsible for exacerbating things.

His other organs were now at risk as well and he'd entered a distressing cycle that would unfortunately continue and lead to death unless Kellen allowed them to intervene with an LVAD. When we were alone again I knew he expected me to try to talk him into getting it one last time, but since I was sure my plea would fall on deaf ears I kept the words to myself.

Instead I closed my eyes and imagined a scenario where he was less stubborn and loved the potential for a future as much as he said he loved me. I must have had my eyes closed for longer than I thought because him squeezing my hand suddenly made them fly back open almost in confusion.

Even without searching for it I could see the pain on his face at the letdown of the whole situation. He had been so hopeful and vulnerable all day thinking that it would be the first to the rest of his life when it'd actually turned out to just be another reminder that the end was getting nearer.

I told myself to be strong for him and did all I could to keep it together, but the weak smile he forced for my benefit only served to trigger my true feelings. He welcomed me back into bed then let me soak his hospital gown with my salty tears until it was time for him to be transferred to a different room.

We hadn't said anything to each other the whole time so I was surprised to hear the emotion in his voice when he asked the nurse if we could have a few more minutes together. During that time I foolishly let him convince me to go home.

He claimed I needed to eat, sleep and be well rested enough to come see him the next day when we could watch the new episode of *Married At First Sight*. He also made me promise not to worry, something we both knew I wouldn't do, but I said I would try anyway before we pressed our lips together.

It lacked the passion needed to call it a full on kiss, but it was just as comforting and loving as any of the other hundreds he'd given me over the last few weeks. If I would have known for sure that it would be our last though…I would have done all that I could to muster up that passion.

I felt like I had barely blinked all night let alone closed my eyes enough to actually fall asleep, but somehow I'd relaxed enough for it to happen. Sleeping in Kellen's bed, in our bed, alone for the first time was something that I didn't want to get used to already though so I still beat the sun up. I was right back there when visiting hours started like I'd planned, but I wasn't allowed in right away because the doctors were in with him.

After about an hour of sitting on my hands, I dialed Kellen's phone directly a couple times to see what was going on, but each call went straight to voicemail. That didn't immediately cause any concern for me, but a team of doctors down the hall exiting the room I knew he was in got the job done.

Despite the charge nurse asking me to remain seated and wait until I was called, I didn't stop walking until I saw his face. He was still lying in bed just like I had left him, but it was obvious that something had to be wrong because there were several machines surrounding him and lots of miscellaneous beeping.

I walked over to get a closer look to make sure that he was sleeping as peacefully as he seemed to be but was interrupted by the same nurse and a white coat who had been summoned to stop me from entering.

"What the hell happened to him and why wasn't I contacted?" I asked, not even trying to hide how I felt about them being on my heels when clearly something more important was going on in there.

"Are you a friend or relative of Mr. Turner's?" the white coat asked a little too calm for my liking because my nerves were shot the second I'd seen him so I needed everybody else to be on edge too.

"I'm his wife," I said even though I had just conveniently left my ring at home. I could tell she didn't believe me because she looked to the nurse for confirmation before I told her to just check his emergency contact forms.

After realizing her mistake she tried to sprinkle a little compassion in her voice only it didn't make a difference to me. I just wanted to know why he was still asleep through the commotion and why there were so many machines hooked up to him.

My mind hadn't even thought of the word coma until she kept assuring me that he wasn't actually in one. She emphasized that he was just heavily sedated to allow his body time to rest and let the machines temporarily do the work for him until he got stronger...if he got stronger.

Hearing that *if* caused me to lose the last few marbles I had left. This whole thing had gone on for far too long and I wasn't having it anymore. I wasn't just going to sit there and let him die. I hadn't gotten around to changing my IDs yet, but I was a Turner now and I decided to throw my weight around and act like one.

"You have to implant the LVAD now. Before you wake him up."

"We've gone over that option with your husband for the last year and he was very clear that he didn't consider it compatible with the way he wanted to live."

"But isn't refusing it basically like a suicide attempt? Can't you threaten to put him on a psych hold to make him do it or something?" I asked hoping I didn't look as desperate as I sounded in case she had the authority to lock me up somewhere instead.

"It's a bit more complicated than that. As long as patients are deemed mentally sound and understand the consequences of their decision then there's nothing we can do."

"So that's it? You would really let him die knowing that there's something you can do?"

"Mrs. Turner I sympathize with you, but Mr. Turner left his final wishes in writing and it would be unethical for us to override that decision just because we don't understand his reasoning."

"You actually wouldn't be overriding anything because he'd recently changed his mind about it all. We just hadn't gotten around to updating everything with the wedding and honeymoon and then setting up house."

She knew I was lying. I knew I was lying. Hell the fly that kept buzzing around the room knew I was lying, but since I was his wife, default next of kin, and his power of health and attorney there was literally nothing she could say that could stop me from my decision.

"Are you willing to sign a document stating that Mr. Turner told you that he'd reconsidered his previous decision about the LVAD?" she asked after giving me an *I'm not getting fired for you* look and I knew that if anything went left to leave her out of it.

"I'll do you one better. I'll bring in our family attorney to find out why you're still standing here and not preparing to implant my husband's lifesaving device now that you have permission to," I said doing my best impression of the kind of woman I imagined Kellen's mama to be from pictures.

She left without another word and I prayed like hell that she didn't call my bluff. I knew for sure I had met Kellen's lawyer at the wedding, but I didn't remember the man's face let alone his name after meeting so many people in one day.

All of that was the least of my worries though. Saving Kellen's life was the only thing on my mind even though I knew he would hate me for it. I tried to rationalize it by thinking at least he would be alive to have feelings at all, but I really didn't know how I would cope if he actually hated me.

What if he divorced me?

The second I was asked to leave the room I felt the temperature getting warmer and immediately knew what it was. I sat in the waiting room for a minute and tried to quell the incoming panic attack, but without my permission it eventually got the best of me.

I put my head in my lap and tried to breathe through it, but a cold hand on my shoulder made me look up. It was *Lena Bean-a!* I had called her that when we were kids, but the memory had literally escaped me until that very second. I couldn't have gotten the words out if I tried to so I didn't try to. I just threw my arms around her and cried like I had never cried before.

Eight hours went by before the entire procedure was completed. I was a nervous wreck the whole time and I found it ironic that the person who was best at calming me down was also the person I was worrying about.

During that time I read everything I could on the pros of getting the device implanted. There were dozens and dozens, but knowing him my biggest selling point would be the big increase in stamina. And if he still wanted to do it with me I swore that I would let him lick me wherever he wanted with no complaints. More than anything though I just wanted him to still love me when he woke up.

I wouldn't know it for a while though because he was deep under after the surgery and they said it would be at least over night until he came to. It was actually around noon the next day and I knew because I had been there at eight sharp waiting for him to open his eyes. He was in the cardiac ICU and there were so many machines attached to him I could barely see his face, but the sound he made when he looked at me let me know that he could see mine.

I could see that he was confused about where he was as he tried to sit up but couldn't because he wasn't strong enough yet. He must've felt the tubing or the device rubbing up against him because he went to grab at it next.

"No. No. No. Don't touch anything!" I shrieked before running to press the call button for the nurse just to be safe.

I looked down at him as I prepared to step away from all the machines and I saw several tears fall from his eyes when he realized what was going on.

"Kellen, I'm so sorry and you have my permission to hate me forever, but I just had to," I said quickly since help was coming any second now. I knew his mouth had to be dry so I told him not to speak, not that he could have anyway with his breathing tube still in.

I watched from a distance as they did more postop screenings and tests to make sure he was okay. His breathing was instantly almost normal again when they removed his tube and sitting up was a breeze with the help of the techs in the room. Talking was still a bit difficult though because he had been under so much anesthesia and sedation medication before that.

When we were nearly alone again he motioned for me to stop the last tech before she could walk out of the door because he needed help sitting up and brushing his teeth. I thought it was odd until he then motioned for me to come closer to kiss him….at least I'd thought it was to kiss him. More tears poured from his eyes as he slowly mouthed words against my lips.

"I could never hate you. I love you more than life, but I told you I didn't want this."

"And I told you not to wait on me. Now we're even."

CLOCKING OUT
SEPTEMBER 20TH - DECEMBER 5TH
13

"I guess we can be enemies some other lifetime because I would rather spend the rest of this one just loving you."

Kellen Turner had every right to be angry with me...and for a while he was. But besides him loving me more than enough not to stay that way, he finally admitted to himself that he would have done the exact same thing if he was losing me.

Him being literally forced into continuing to live was still a complex situation though and it made us both go through the full range of emotions. I finally got back around to my therapy sessions and he also decided to give it a try to process the magnitude of what he'd been through.

He let me stay by his side during his three week hospital stay, but the moment he was released he had professional caretakers waiting to help him day and night so that I wouldn't be overwhelmed. And true to his word he sent me back to the diner to do the renovations I'd always dreamed of because he said he wanted me to live for the both of us since he couldn't at the moment.

I felt guilty about not being glued to his side all day like I'd wanted to be, but even I had to admit that we did need some time apart after how quickly and intensely our relationship had come together. We were basically tethered to each other night and day for a month and under so much pressure from his looming death that a healthy break was more than needed to breathe.

By day I inhaled and perfected being a girlboss, but I made sure to save just enough energy to exhale and catch up with him before we went to bed at night. And watching him get a little bit closer to the man I had fallen in love with was one of the most beautiful things I had ever seen before.

Leaning on Lena had practically become a lifestyle for me over the last few years so after everything had finally calmed down I decided to treat my favorite cousin the same way she would have treated me if the roles were reversed. Along with her new title as manager she got a hefty raise and a well-deserved vacation on me.

The thing she appreciated the most though was when she got back in town and saw that I had taken a few feet from the diner's men's room to expand the ladies' room. That seed of expansion was just the beginning though because it inspired me to open up my old apartment and make the entire upstairs a part of the venue.

Getting permits for everything on such short notice was not easy in the least bit, but in this city when you had the money and the connections that came with the last name Turner, people kind of just got out of your way and let you do whatever you wanted. Just when I was about to start confirming my long-held belief that money really did buy happiness, I had to add an asterisk because for some people it just paid for a nicer grave.

I had never quite gotten all the details, not that I really needed them to know what'd happened, but apparently Florida ended up not being as relaxing as Jimmy would have hoped it'd be. According to Paula with the money he'd gotten from the sale of the diner, which was well over market value, Jimmy and his newfound riches had been cutting up in Florida strip clubs from the moment they got there.

Her story was that he was the victim of a robbery gone wrong since he had been having fun and carrying around lots of cash, but the locals said he had groped the wrong woman and was dealt with accordingly. I knew I should have felt something about my uncle's death, but it certainly wasn't going to be bad because it seemed fitting for all the storms he'd caused women just like me over the years.

The strangest thing about the situation was that his death seemed to coincide with the removal of his name from the building. Jimmy the man and Jimmy's diner were both no more within a couple days of one another. I didn't know if it was symbolic in some way, but luckily he had stored Mae's old sign all these years so I had it polished up and reinstalled in no time.

Going to work on my first day at Mae's Kitchen for the grand reopening was one for the books. Everything was either brand spanking new or shined up so well that it looked that way. I even finally had the old jukebox rocking again.

Lena immediately got to work posting a bunch of pictures for the new social media accounts that she'd started for the diner. It wasn't until then that I realized just how many social media worthy events I'd missed cashing in on for likes that year because I had been too busy actually living in the moment.

I had become owner of the diner, moved into a luxury high-rise condo, fallen in love and gotten married without so much as even a single humble-brag post. I guess that was how it was supposed to be though.

Now I was no longer a waitress and certainly not a cook, but for the day I put on one of the new and improved uniforms because for one very special customer I opened up a little early and became both. The familiar bell dinging above the door let me know that Kellen and his wide smile were right on schedule so I ran to set his two toast and a warm cup of coffee at his counter seat.

Yes that counter seat…

"How did you know I wasn't going to order something else?"

"Because other than water you know I'm not letting you have anything else on this menu."

"Well can I at least get some butter and jam on them then?" he asked making me remember when Jenna had suggested he do the same thing months ago.

The devilish smile he suddenly wore let me know that he'd intended to take me back to the one moment of jealousy he'd witnessed from me so I moved both out of reach for him.

He kissed his teeth before looking around at everything for the first time as I came from behind the counter to show off the new uniform. He nodded his approval of the pants, but of course he had to be a man and remind me how much he *loved* my legs in the old one.

I almost let it slip that I had saved one just for him, but I decided to let it remain a surprise until we could actually put it to use. As if he was reading my mind he reminded me that he was headed to see his specialist to officially be cleared for *strenuous exercise* so working the late shift wouldn't be an option tonight.

He needed to be able to walk up two flights of stairs without being too winded, but I had made it three just to be on the safe side. That man must have really wanted to be with me again because he had been doing four flights for a week and the doctor said he'd had one of the best recoveries she'd ever seen.

Eventually the first real customers of the day came in and after I got them seated I went to walk Kellen out. December had just begun, but you wouldn't have known it by the weather which seemed more like early fall. I still had him wrapped up in all the layers though because I wasn't taking any chances on him even getting so much as a runny nose on my watch.

"Hey! You stiffed me on my tip," I complained when I realized that he had basically dined and dashed on me too.

"I'll give it to you when I come back later for lunch," he promised before lowering himself to peck my lips.

"Uh oh. Am I gonna have to limit how many days you can stop by again already?" I teased him about how thirsty he'd been for me back in the beginning.

"You could try, but my wife owns this place now so I can come here as much as I want to."

"Your wife? Last time I checked you were waiting on me to get my shit together."

"Yeah well you were taking too long and I'm a hot commodity," he said playing along before straightening up. "But nowhere near as hot as you are. I'm so proud of you. You got it looking even better than the old pictures in there."

"I know! Just wait until you see upstairs. You wouldn't even be able to tell it was an apartment before," I said excitedly then rambled until I noticed him just watching me with that smile I loved so much.

"You know I just realized that when I first walked through those doors, I was alone and dying and now coming out the other side I've got you and a whole new life to look forward to."

"Hm. Maybe there's something magical about them?" I suggested playfully as I looked over my shoulder at the deep red doors that had never matched anything inside.

"Yeah maybe or maybe it's just that you walk through them every day," he said sweetly.

We went to hug goodbye but hesitated because we were still overly cautious and getting adjusted to his LVAD always being there. He'd chosen the vest option because it went nearly undetectable under his suits so it was really easy for me to forget sometimes.

I leaned against the diner's doors for a second as I watched Kellen prepare to leave and thought back to our first time standing out there when he brought up waiting for me. That moment and the rest of our firsts had occurred during the worst storm season of our lives, but instead of looking for an umbrella we had just taught each other how to have fun in the rain.

The fun didn't stop when the clouds cleared though and before long our two imperfect heartbeats had somehow created a perfectly healthy little third one. And after searching far and wide for a fitting name, we decided to do like our folks had done and just combined ours.

Her birth certificate said Kelly Bell Turner, but for short we mostly just called her Kel.

Waiting On Wendy

TANZANIA GLOVER

FOLLOW ME

Thanks for reading! If you don't want to miss out on any updates about future works of mine then find me on all social media platforms as TanSaidWhat, sign up for my mailing list, and join my reading group Turning The Page With Tanzania Glover.

Visit www.tanzaniaglover.com

And if the cover art took your breath away as much as it did mine, check out the talented artist Sia Tania! Thank you so much for bringing this couple to life!

9 798987 494233